Meet the officers of the Mountain Country K-9 Unit series and their brave K-9 partners

Officers: Michael Tanner and Isla Jimenez

K-9 Partners: Bogi the Belgian Malinois

Assignment: Safeguard a K-9 pursued by dangerous criminals

Officers: Sully Briggs and Cara Haines

K-9 Partners: Deacon the Doberman pinscher and Mocha the K-9 in training

Assignment: Rescue a targeted witness before the mob finds her

With over seventy books published and millions in print, **Lenora Worth** writes award-winning romance and romantic suspense. Three of her books finaled in the ACFW Carol Awards, and her Love Inspired Suspense novel *Body of Evidence* became a *New York Times* bestseller. Her novella in *Mistletoe Kisses* made her a *USA TODAY* bestselling author. Lenora goes on adventures with her retired husband, Don, and enjoys reading, baking and shopping...especially shoe shopping.

Katy Lee writes suspenseful romances that thrill and inspire. She believes every story should stir and satisfy the reader—from the edge of their seat. A native New Englander, Katy loves to knit warm woolly things. She enjoys traveling the side roads and exploring the locals' hideaways. A homeschooling mom of three competitive swimmers, Katy often writes from the stands while cheering them on. Visit Katy at katyleebooks.com.

Christmas
K-9 Guardians

LENORA WORTH
KATY LEE

LOVE INSPIRED SUSPENSE
INSPIRATIONAL ROMANCE

Special thanks and acknowledgment are given to Lenora Worth and Katy Lee for their contributions to the Mountain Country K-9 Unit miniseries.

LOVE INSPIRED®SUSPENSE
INSPIRATIONAL ROMANCE

Recycling programs
for this product may
not exist in your area.

ISBN-13: 978-1-335-48392-8

Christmas K-9 Guardians

Copyright © 2024 by Harlequin Enterprises ULC

Perilous Christmas Pursuit
Copyright © 2024 by Harlequin Enterprises ULC

Lethal Holiday Hideout
Copyright © 2024 by Harlequin Enterprises ULC

Love Inspired
22 Adelaide St. West, 41st Floor
Toronto, Ontario M5H 4E3, Canada
www.LoveInspired.com

Printed in U.S.A.

CONTENTS

PERILOUS CHRISTMAS PURSUIT

Lenora Worth

To my puppy Bogi. Thank you for the doggy kisses and the unconditional love.

Keep thy heart with all diligence;
for out of it are the issues of life.
—*Proverbs* 4:23

ONE

"Hi, Granny, I'm almost done. How's it going?"

Isla Jimenez held the phone to her ear and glanced at the white-and-black clock on the wall of her downstairs tech fortress at the Elk Valley, Wyoming, Police Department. Almost eight o'clock. She always liked the near silence at the end of the day after most people had gone home. Her brain worked better when she could be alone and hear nothing but the thoughts in her head, the kind of silence she'd craved as a child. No one shouting, no one fighting, no one crying in a corner. Group homes were not for the squeamish.

She'd promised her grandmother she'd be home by now. The last home visit from the adoption agency would take place tomorrow and she wanted to finish setting up Enzo's bedroom. He already lived with her as a foster child, but he'd officially become her child if all went well.

She could finally adopt Enzo and make him her own. She already loved the toddler but a few setbacks had kept the red tape of the adoption tied up. She'd had a busy year. As a technical analyst for the police department and the Mountain Country K-9 Unit, she'd helped solve a serial killer cold case. The investigation spanned eight months. During that time, she'd also been targeted by a stalker—a woman from her past who'd tried to defame her to the adoption agency—who'd finally been arrested. With Christmas fast approaching, Isla was ready to put those difficult events behind her.

"Things are good here, honey," her grandmother, Annette, said. "I can't wait for you to get home so we can finally celebrate. I'm going to be the best *abuela* in the world."

"You are already that, Granny Annie," Isla replied, glad she lived across the street from the station. She'd been a foster child all of her life and when she'd aged out, by the grace of God, Annette, the maternal grandmother she'd never known, had been waiting for her with an offer she couldn't refuse. A home and funding for college.

"I am, aren't I?" her ever-feisty grandmother replied, her bubbly laugh sending sweet chimes out over the airways. "Hurry home. I made flan for dessert."

Isla's favorite. Having her grandmother move in with her to help with Enzo did have its perks. Isla had a lot to celebrate this Christmas. The excitement of finally being Enzo's mother kept her going even when she was exhausted. Thankful that her dream had come true, she didn't need anything else for Christmas. Having Granny and Enzo with her, after the year she'd been through, gave her the peace she'd prayed for so long. Now she could truly relax and enjoy this final step.

She closed her files, saving them in an encrypted cloud. Before she shut everything down, she did one last check—she liked things neat—then grabbed a small laptop and some flash drives so she could finish up a few files before taking a week off. Always on call, she planned to enjoy some time with Granny Annie and Enzo over the next few days. Quiet time, so precious, to cuddle and dream of gifts and goodies.

Heading toward the elevator, she stopped and went still when she heard footsteps echoing from the stairs. Who could be coming down to her lab without warning so late at night?

"Isla, you're still here."

"Michael?" The local vet took care of the department's K-9 officer dogs and did a great job at it. Handsome and quiet, his hazel eyes always alert, his hair always needing a comb, he never had much to say, and he had no reason to come looking for her. And yet that shiver of awareness made her glad to see him. "What are you doing here?"

Then she saw the massive dog standing like a stone lion with him. "Hey there, fellow. Don't tell me you want to work in the lab?"

Neither the dog nor the man responded to her humor.

Silence. They both stood with guarded gazes, the tension around them palpable. What was going on?

Michael Tanner filled her electronic space like an oak tree spreading over a rose garden. Granny would call him *fine*. Nice-looking and muscular, with a stoic expression that showed he meant business. And so did the beautiful black-and-tan dog with him. A Malinois.

"I need your help," he said. "In a technical way."

Trying to make things light because she really wanted to get home, she said, "As pickup lines go, that one is unique."

"I'm serious." His gaze flickered from her to the stairs behind him. "Can I come inside?"

Why had she even said that about pickup lines? Lifting her shoulders and chin, she said, "I was about to go home."

Michael ran a hand over his thick gold-brown hair, which matched the dog's fur almost perfectly. "Bogi is in danger. He has a target on his back."

He nodded toward the dog and said nothing else.

"Is this Bogi?"

"Yes, aka Bogi the Narc Shark. Highly trained in drug detection, but he's an all-purpose K-9. He recently sniffed out a shipment of fentanyl and other drugs worth over ten million dollars. A raid down in Texas."

"Wow, impressive," she said, offering her knuckles toward the dog. Bogi gave her a brown-eyed stare down but didn't sniff her hand. More than highly trained. Like lightning on a leash. The big dog shifted his head, the leather collar around his neck jiggling.

She glanced back at Michael. "So how did he wind up in Wyoming?"

"Because his work is so impressive, someone wants him dead," Michael replied, his words low and whispery. "I'm supposed to be hiding him, but these people always find what they want."

"These people?" Isla's heart rate pulsed some heavy beats. How many times had she helped find and put away *these people*? "Define that, please?"

"Cartel people," Michael explained. "It's a long story and I don't have much time. It's top secret—me having him in the first place. But I think they've found out and I can't reach my contact in Texas."

"As in, the cartel people are looking for you two?" she asked, her brain moving into gear even though her imagination created creepy scenarios. "Were you followed here?"

"I don't think so," Michael replied in a voice that made him sound like an undercover spy. "I can't be sure, but the place is like a ghost town tonight what with the holidays coming up. You were my last resort."

"And yet, another great line to win a woman's heart," she said, because she always used sarcasm to hide her fear. And she sometimes blurted out whatever popped into her head. "Get in here, Doc, and let's see what we can find out."

She studied Bogi. "And don't worry, handsome. Sounds like you're a major hero. We'll see what we can find and who we can find to protect you." Glancing at Michael, she said, "I'll need to report this to Chase, of course." When he didn't respond, she went on, "Nora is out of town right now."

The police chief, Nora Quan, had taken a few days off for the holidays.

"They'll both want an explanation."

Chase Rawlston, FBI Special Agent in Charge, and the head of the Mountain Country K-9 Unit, had saved her life when he'd caught Lisa King, a woman who'd been a preteen in the group home where Isla had spent most of her life. Lisa had been her stalker, seeking revenge because she'd blamed Isla for her little brother's disappearance years ago. She'd tried to ruin Isla's credentials and terrorize her into thinking she'd never be able to adopt. It had almost worked, but Chase and the team had watched out for Isla. She trusted him. He'd know what to do for Michael, and she'd help in any way she could. Probably a veterinarian overreacting.

Only, Michael Tanner never overreacted. Some of the team members called him Mr. Cool. Always calm and focused on the animals that came to his clinic, just as he now focused on the trained dog beside him. Isla could feel the tension pinging off him like shell casings pounding the ground. She had to help him. And not because she might have a tiny crush on him. Just part of her job. Or so she told herself.

She'd hurry and call Chase for advice. She couldn't risk getting involved in anything that might mess up what could be her last opportunity to finally adopt Enzo.

Before she could find her phone, however, Michael held up a hand. "Don't make that call yet."

After she gave him a dagger-filled stare, Michael Tanner followed Isla over to the massive desk where she restarted her equipment. He watched as several different screens blinked and churned and sputtered, the bells and whistles of technology humming along at warp speed while his life had come to a complete halt. He considered her the best at tracking down information that could slay dangerous criminals. After all, she'd been put on a task force to hunt a serial killer. She sure didn't need any more danger coming from him.

They barely knew each other, but his gut told him he could trust her. He'd seen the petite, brown-eyed woman in action and he'd always been impressed with her professionalism and her need for justice. She worked fast, too. He could almost see the information he'd given her percolating in her brain. Tonight, he had that same need for justice in mind, and the one person he wanted to talk to couldn't be found. Isla could help. She could locate just about anyone using her tech talents.

But right now she shook her head and glared at him. "What are you saying? I have to alert someone and Chase is the SAC. I report to him when Nora's not around."

"I'm sorry, Isla. I'm trying to keep a low profile, so let's keep this between us for now. All I need is intel on one person—the friend who asked me to do this."

"You're right about this place being deserted," she said, her gaze questioning his every move. "The task force is taking a break, spread out through the whole month, but I still need to report this. I'm taking some time off next week. Monday, I'm signing the official papers to adopt Enzo, and I'm going to enjoy the holidays with him. So let me get you some help before I leave."

He heard the determined inflection in her words. She really wanted to get away from him. Could she sense the danger that surrounded him, the kind of danger that could ruin innocent people's lives? This was why he held friends at bay. He couldn't—shouldn't—have come here.

"I'd heard about that," he said, unable to tell her that someone had tried to break into his clinic. He could handle a fight, no problem. But when it came to animals, he'd go beyond a fight. And he refused to think of those dark days of anger when he looked for the fight and welcomed it. Not now, when Bogi's life depended on Michael keeping his cool.

She pivoted back toward him and Bogi, bristling in an urgent-business mode. "So what happened and what do you need?"

He was about to explain when they heard

an echoing crash overhead. Gunshots on the floor above, followed by a thud. Did an officer on duty get hit? He gave Bogi the silent signal.

"They followed me," he whispered as he glanced over his shoulder. He shouldn't have come here. Now they'd target Isla, too. Grabbing her by the arm, he pushed her toward the stairs. "We have to go. Now."

Isla's eyes widened with a glow of surprise. "Go where? If we're not safe in police headquarters."

He tried to tug her behind a big cabinet.

Isla pulled away, disbelief mixed with traces of fear in her eyes, a gasp escaping her parted lips.

More shots, footsteps hurrying. Then the elevator dinged, and the door slid open to reveal a big man in black with a gun nestled in his hand.

Isla and the man stood face-to-face for a split second while Michael blocked Bogi behind the cabinet. Before the man could do anything, Michael swung around and fired one shot, hitting the intruder in his left shoulder. He fell to the floor.

Isla screamed as Michael dragged her away, Bogi getting between the unconscious man and them, a low growl his only sign of aggression.

"Guard," Michael commanded Bogi. "Isla, don't move."

She gave him a look that shouted at him, then she whirled toward the man bleeding on the floor, but the K-9 stood guard. Michael couldn't explain things right now, but she'd want answers and she deserved to know what was really going on. He'd flipped a switch and she'd witnessed it. No turning back now.

Michael checked the man's pulse. "He'll live, but we have to go."

She shifted back. "Shouldn't we wait until the police come?"

Michael shook his head. "No, we can't. You're not safe. They want Bogi, dead or alive. But mostly dead. And I'm pretty sure they want me, too. Really dead."

"You failed to mention that part," she said, suddenly diving into gathering more equipment. She grabbed electronics she'd need. They both knew to be prepared for anything. But right now, she needed to get out of here.

"Leave it," he said. "We need to go now."

He shoved her toward the outer door while she grabbed her backpack. "I'm taking this," she said in a breathless rush that dared him to argue. "I have one of my secure laptops in here."

"We're gonna need more than electronics," he replied. "My past has finally caught up with me, Isla."

TWO

A thousand thoughts moved through Isla's mind like a gurgling river. Anger and frustration, empathy and understanding, and finally, acceptance and resolve. Michael guided her out of the compound in a way that told her he'd done this before, his body tense, his gaze scanning like a radar zooming in on a target. He told her to put a hand on his shoulder and keep it there. Michael had a gun and a new attitude, now in full commando mode. Something she couldn't grasp right now. Something that made her see why Michael Tanner had intrigued her and made her aware of him each time she'd been around him. Something dangerous, and dark, and disturbing. He was a warrior. He moved with precision, his footsteps light, his grip on her heavy and heated, while they skirted the extreme perimeters of the buildings and parking lots. Bogi followed his every command, sniffing, guarding, watching.

Isla shifted her backpack and wondered since when did an animal doctor know K-9 signals at every turn? Yes, he moved like a trained K-9 handler, like a trained soldier. Maybe he'd worked in that position before becoming a vet? A military position? A lot of veterans came home and found work that involved the police. Or maybe he'd trained so he could be more capable around the dogs?

No. This man—this side of Michael Tanner—showed more than a love of animals. His actions were calculated and deliberate, cautious and determined.

She'd have questions later. But right now, she had to alert someone. "I need to call my grandmother," she said when they were beyond the complex and moving from tree to tree. "She's with Enzo. Really, my house is right there on the corner. We could run over there."

"No," he said, that one word sharper than a knife blade.

Isla stopped in her high-topped turquoise tennis shoes. "What do you mean, no? I have to, Michael. I'm about to sign the adoption papers. In the morning I have one more person coming from the agency to see how things are going. I want to go home."

"They know you're with me," he said, giving her a firm solid-as-a-wall glance. "They'll do whatever it takes to get to Bogi."

Isla's heart raced ahead while she tried to comprehend things. Darkness permeated her with the kind of fear she'd fought against most of her life. The kind that had made her hide in corners and cower in her bed late at night. She didn't cower these days. All in for justice, she'd learned to push fear to the far corners of her mind.

But now she had someone else to protect. Enzo. "They'll try to harm me or my family?"

"Yes," he said, glancing around. "We need transportation."

Isla's heart pierced against her ribs, her

throat went dry. "My car's at my house, where I am going right now."

Michael held her arm, his fingers like steel against her skin. "No. We need to keep moving."

"I'm not going anywhere until you explain about your past. Are you kidnapping me?"

"No," he said, his own frustration showing in the dull glow of a winter moon. "No," he said in a softer voice. "I'm trying to protect you. Turn your phone off. Now."

Isla shook her head, disbelief tearing through her soul. "I have to warn my grandmother. She moved in after we renovated my place because of the fire. She and Enzo are at my house, waiting for me."

She glanced down the street to where Christmas lights sparkled on her front porch, her mind searching like a laptop engine for a way out of this. She wanted to be in that little cottage, where a fresh-smelling tree stood decorated with colorful bulbs and trinkets, and gifts were wrapped and waiting, where the smell of cinnamon and roasted pecans would fill the air. Enzo's first Christmas with her. She couldn't miss that.

But Michael held her, his whisper low and raspy like steel grating against concrete. "If you go home, they'll both be in the line of fire, Isla. It's safer if we get you away from here as quickly as possible."

Isla dug in her boot heels. "I can't leave them."

"We'll get some protection on your home, once we're out of here. This is no joke. I got clearance from high up to protect Bogi. He's got a bounty on his head. I'm supposed to be hiding him and now we've been compromised." He gave her a dangerously determined stare. "And because I came to you for help, that means you've been compromised, too."

"Then *let* me help," she said, thinking he spoke like a commander. "Shots were fired at the police department, so right about now they'll find that wounded man in my lab. They'll want explanations. The cameras will show you and I leaving together. I need to get an encrypted message to Chase. He'll go after whoever is trying to get to Bogi, but first he'll want answers. I want answers, too." She watched his reaction—nothing. Just a stone wall hiding a fortress. "Like right now."

A lift of his chin gave her a hint that he'd heard her. Sirens whined through the night. "It's out on the radio now. That should scare them off for a while. I'll give you answers when I know you're safe."

"Meantime, I'm calling Chase."

He held her arm. "It's still too risky to make your call. Chase knows me, Isla. He'll understand I had to get you out of there."

Isla shivered, the adrenaline wearing off to leave her shaking in her wool peacoat and flower-embossed jeans. She'd worked on hundreds of criminal cases, but she'd never been thrown into the middle of one. But that man could have killed Michael and taken Bogi. She'd been a distraction, at least.

Watching her, he finally said, "Let me get you somewhere safe and I'll explain. Then you can send your encrypted message. Meantime, that wounded man can answer to whoever finds him first. If he's still alive."

She didn't argue but as soon as she could, she would get away from him and his need to protect her. She couldn't go through this kind of thing again, this being afraid, running from the shadows, always trying to find her way to peace. She had to stay out of trouble for Enzo's sake.

They'd made it three blocks south of the police department when a dark SUV came barreling toward them, its big wheels bouncing and growling like an angry tiger as the driver accelerated and headed straight for them.

Michael pushed her down into the leftover early snow and held his body over hers. Bogi dropped in front of them, his head up, his ears out. For a brief moment, Isla felt a shield of protection, something she'd never felt before, something comforting and dangerous all at the same time.

The truck sped by, then did a swift turn, swerving around toward where they were hiding behind a huge mass of evergreen shrubbery. That ended the brief whiff of protection she'd felt.

Isla held close to Michael, bracing herself. The truck would hit them and probably kill both of them. And what would happen to Bogi? What would happen to Granny and Enzo?

She had to stop this. But before she even moved an inch, Michael rolled over and pulled out what looked like a slender grenade from his jacket pocket, his finger tugging at the clip.

Then he threw it toward the roaring truck.

Isla waited for the explosion, bracing herself. But no explosion came. A bright flash of blinding light followed by a huge puff of gray smoke that filled the truck and cut off the driver's ability to see. A flash-bang. Military grade.

She lay frozen until Michael lifted her into the air and said, "Run."

She ran, glancing back as the truck hit the tree and knocked out a light post. When they were about a half mile away he finally stopped to drag her into an alley, Bogi never leaving his side.

After Michael scanned the street, he spotted a hole-in-the wall bar and grill. "Let's go inside there and sit in the back."

"What if they find us?"

"We run out the back into the alley across from this one."

She took a breath and turned to the man who'd ruined her night. Shivers slipped along her spine like fingers trying to grab at her. "Who are you really, Michael Tanner? And don't even try to lie to me. I have enough equipment in my bag to dig deep into that past you mentioned, and I'm pretty sure it's either military or you're a trained assassin." Grabbing him by the collar, she added, "But I'd rather hear the truth from you, here and now. Or I'm walking."

Michael gave her a fierce stare, the shadows around them making him look like a prowling lion. "That would be a big mistake."

Michael didn't know where to begin. He could have hidden out somewhere until the heat was off. Instead, he'd rushed out without a plan, his one goal to get to these people before they got to him. Someone had used Bogi as a lure to reveal Michael's whereabouts, to flush him out. Not that he'd been deliberately hiding. But he had kept a low profile and tried to stay out of trouble.

Now trouble had found him.

As they sat in a grimy booth by the back door of the dank-smelling, crowded bar, he said, "We need transportation."

People gave them surprised looks but Bogi wasn't kicked out. The staff didn't seem to care one way or the other and the few scrappy patrons didn't even take a second glance.

Isla did a scan of the few working red lights on the twisted strings of Christmas ornaments and the sad little fake tree that hovered dangerously close to falling off the corner of the battered bar top. Not exactly romantic, not that he had any romantic thoughts at the moment. He'd always liked Isla and now he admired her, too. She didn't back down and she would get away from him if she found an opportunity.

"Don't worry about a getaway car yet," she replied, her pretty eyes fired up and angry. "You need to tell me the truth. I can't run off with you and leave everything behind."

"I'll make sure things are okay with Enzo," he said. "You'll get to adopt him."

"Wow, you have that much power? What kind of animal doctor are you?"

"The kind that goes all out to protect an innocent K-9 officer dog, a war dog," he said after he'd given Bogi some water from a paper cup he gotten from a waitress. Then he scratched the dog's neck just over his thick collar. "It's a long story."

Isla gave him a sarcastic stare. "I've got nothing but time, thanks to you."

A spitfire, but petite and nice-looking, her eyes dark and open like an unexplored cavern. Only he didn't have time to explore caverns or figure out women. And she was right. He'd pretty much ruined her time off. Depending on how this played out, he might ruin her life.

So he decided to talk. She could guide him through the truth of this maze by following the online footprints. He had his suspicions, but he wouldn't divulge them yet. He needed the kind of proof that couldn't be disputed.

They ordered sodas. "Are you hungry?" he asked her, thinking she had to be.

"No. I can't eat. Too wound up. Start talking, Doc."

He sent the waitress away with their drink orders. Time to level with Isla. He owed her the truth.

"I started out at Lackland Air Force Base in Texas. As you probably know, it's a joint base with Fort Sam Houston Army Base. I've always had a love for animals, so I immediately applied for the Military Working Dogs program at JBSA."

"Wow," she said, filling in the blanks. "Joint Base San Antonio. So you trained with the Army? That's an impressive program. Most of our dogs come from there." Glaring at him, she asked, "Why haven't I heard this before? Maybe because your background is on a need-to-know basis?"

"That's right," he said, watching the door for any suspicious customers. Although most everyone in this dive looked suspicious. "Bogi and I trained together then went into security forces, part of the military special ops program. We worked for the Department of Defense, doing two tours in the Middle East, searching for explosives and narcotics. Bogi is an all-purpose K-9, trained to track anything or anybody. He's good with finding bombs and drugs."

The dog lifted his head but remained settled near Michael's feet, his nose constantly lifting in the air.

"And you?" she asked. "You're obviously trained for something dangerous, and you have a past that doesn't include being a veterinarian."

Michael lowered his head. "You're right. I have a…past that I've tried to forget. My last few months on tour, we were sent on a dangerous mission that went bad. People died on both sides. I got injured, so I decided to leave the military. Which is why I went to Plan B—becoming a veterinarian." He shrugged. "It keeps me close to the K-9s and because of what I went through as a military handler, I can help them both physically and mentally."

He couldn't give her details of his past

assignments. That would involve confidential information and put her in more danger. If she knew the truth—all of the truth— she would walk right out of here as she'd threatened.

Isla sat silent for a moment, then said, "I know there's more to that story. I have enough compassion to know most military people don't like to open their wounds to anyone, especially the emotional wounds." She took a deep breath. "And I'm sensing both you and Bogi have an emotional bond."

He tried not to flinch. "You might say that, yeah."

"So how did you wind up here?"

"I saw an ad on a job site. The part about working with K-9s got my attention," he replied. "I needed to start fresh, away from Texas and the memories, and because I had enough experience on both ends of the spectrum, both in handling and providing medical attention to the dogs, I felt like God had given me a nudge. Bogi had moved on with another handler, but his partner got killed only a few months after they were together. I kept in touch through a friend stationed back at JBSA. Bogi suffered even more trauma after his partner's death, and the base brass wanted to put him down."

"No." Isla glanced at the dog sitting there so noble and calm, so alert and sure. "He's a hero." He saw resolve dawning in her light brown eyes. "You said he got hired out for one last mission—to bring down a drug cartel. So, when he found that supply and cut off a big chunk of their income, the cartel put out a hit on him. They won't forget that. They'll kill him to make a point. We can't let that happen."

"Yes, they'll make him an example to scare others," Michael said. "Human or animal, they'll make sure someone pays."

He didn't tell her the rest of his suspicions. Bogi had been handpicked for that last mission because he'd been trained to be aggressive at sniffing out drugs. One last chance to prove himself or end it all in a noble way if he got injured or killed?

Michael couldn't be sure, but stranger plans had gone down. And something about this whole thing—him being singled out to protect Bogi—smelled rotten. But how could he say no? He still did contract work here and there as needed, and this was one of those times. He'd do anything to protect Bogi.

"Because you came to me for deep dives into the dark web—these people will want me dead now, too. I'm beginning to see the picture."

Michael opened his mouth to speak, then quickly hushed when the creaking double doors swung open and two men in black leather jackets walked in and scanned the room. He gave Bogi the silent command, then put a finger to his lips and dropped a ten-dollar bill on the table. Motioning Isla toward the door closest to them, he tugged her up and into his arms while he tried to shield both her and Bogi.

"Lean on me as if we're leaving together. Like a couple."

Shock covered Isla's face as he held her tight, their backs turned away from the men. Michael watched out of the corner of his eyes as he hurried her and the dog out.

The men searched back and forth. Michael glanced back and locked eyes with one of them. "They've spotted us. Run, Isla."

THREE

Isla ran for her life. Not only did she run from those massive men who'd come into the bar, but she needed to get away from the way she'd felt when Michael had swept her into his arms and held her close. Could she ever breathe properly again?

A big truck turned down the alleyway as they slipped off to the right and sprinted as fast as they could to the next street. Isla's heart raced and her backpack felt like a load of heavy stones hitting against her backbone, but she couldn't leave it here on the streets. It was her connection—their connection—to find someone out there to help them.

"They must have trackers on one of us," Michael whispered, his breath huffing as he searched his clothes. "It might be difficult for them to do, but they'll keep coming even if we find any bugs."

Isla's mind went spinning ahead on all cylinders, her thoughts sputtering like a print-out spitting out of a machine while she checked herself and her backpack.

"Nothing," she said. "I can't believe this."

Michael tugged her close. "I'll get you home soon, Isla. I promise."

"I don't know if you can promise me anything at this point."

He put his hands on her elbows, his expression deeply etched with a dangerous determination. "I got you into this and now it will be up to me to get you out. Bogi and I can do that together. I promise. And I always keep my promises."

Still stunned by the way Michael was holding her, Isla tried to stay calm. She had handled delicate, intricate evidence for years, but this was different. This *evidence* chased a man and dog, trying to kill them, and her, too, for that matter. How could she find a way to finish what Bogi had started and end this evil cartel? Not just for her sake or Michael's and Bogi's sake. But for all the people out there addicted to drugs. Hadn't she seen enough of that living in a group home?

How can I make a difference? How can I go up against a cartel?

And still keep the life she'd always dreamed of.

She said a prayer, asking for intervention. *I can't lose Enzo. I can give him the love he needs, a good home, a safe place to grow up. I'm so close. But I can't get myself out of this. I need help, Lord. Michael and Bogi need Your help.*

Could she really help Michael? Doubts started tugging her down as they weaved from street to street, hiding behind buildings, trees and bushes. When would this end? When could she sit down and catch her breath and let Chase know their situation? He'd have a team together in no time and get them out of this mess.

Michael tugged her toward a busy area shrouded in mushrooming oak trees. "I'm going to rent a car."

She saw a shabby car rental building on

the corner and nodded. Then her mind went to work. "In your name?"

"I have other names," he admitted. "I'm still backstopped for various reasons."

Backstopped—meaning he had a whole fake background set up in case anyone vetted him. Which meant he probably still did some freelance work for the DOD or the CIA. Contract work. He considered this contract work. Was he a spy? Or an agent on call? All this time, she'd seen him come and go at headquarters and never once did she imagine this quiet, intense man had a hidden past. And was a hero, too. He couldn't accept that right now. Or maybe, he needed one more fight to become a hero again, to right those wrongs from the mission that had gone bad?

She wouldn't press him any more for now. He'd carried his secrets so well, he had everyone fooled. Or did he?

"Does Chase know everything about you, Michael?" she asked as they hurried toward the blinking lights of the auto rental place.

He didn't respond at first. He was on high alert and she should be, too. Bogi mastered the art, doing his thing, looking aware and intense. Trained. Dangerous. They were both trained and dangerous, and they moved together like one, their shadows merging in the dark night like a giant superpower.

"Michael?"

He finally turned before they went inside the building. "As you said, he is the SAC and the team he put together will continue to work closely with the locals. He knows what he knows, and that's all I can say."

"You don't have to say anything else. Chase won't reveal anything. He's solid."

"I know," Michael said. "He's the only one I can trust right now, besides you."

"You trust me?"

"Only if you'll trust me," he shot back. "Let's get this done so we can be on our way."

She followed him into the dingy fluorescent-lit office, but she wanted badly to ask him where exactly they would be going.

He didn't know where to take her. Finally, he decided he'd rely on one of the safe houses he'd used before when things got dicey. He thought he'd left the worst behind but being a contracted undercover operative for years had left a lot of enemies along the path. Could one of them be tied in with the cartel?

But why? Which one? Revenge? Boredom? Playing games to mess with his head? Or someone going all vigilante on him?

Midnight, and the rental car wasn't the best. A small economy model which used less gas, but a tight squeeze for Bogi in the back. The big dog kept scratching at his collar. For now, Isla and Bogi were safe.

"What's your plan?" she asked, sounding defeated as she accepted what had happened. Her tone went low and raw, the rage she had to be feeling hissing like a live wire with each word.

She'd never forgive him for this.

"Right now, to get you and Bogi off the streets and then you can let Chase know you're with me and safe." He checked the mirrors and did a zigzag across the town center and then out onto a less traveled road with foothills and deep ravines on each side.

Isla kept glancing around. "Think he'll buy that? He's probably reviewed the station's video. He'll see you coming down to my lab, and then shooting that man and forcing me out the door."

"He has to know I got you out of there for a reason. He knows me. Knows how I operate."

"Too bad I didn't know that before now, too."

Michael wanted to explain more, but he had to focus. "Look, I do what I have to do when things need to get done. And right now, this is my mission. To protect this K-9. And you."

She stared at him as if he'd turned to stone. "I think you and I should sit down and come up with a plan *together*. I turned my phone off. I'm sure Chase will have figured out why I disappeared with you by now. He'll likely have put a patrol on my house. But I have my own obligations and I can't risk getting caught up with a cartel.

I need to find a way to get that cartel off our backs." She let out a sigh. "I can't even believe I said that."

"I'm sorry," he replied. "I thought if I could do some digging—the kind that needs to stay off the record—I could quickly access the situation and make a solid decision. I must be getting rusty."

"I'm sorry, too. You're obviously trained to avoid such things. Whatever happened to you before, you've let your guard down now. You're doing work you love. I can't fault you on that, but what stirred this up?"

She had him there. "I trusted the wrong people," he said. "I won't make that mistake again."

"Do you bring people here often?" Isla asked Michael when they entered the little cabin nestled at the bottom of a stone-faced ridge near the Laramie Mountain foothills.

"Only when necessary," he said. "It's off the beaten path but it has great internet and cell reception."

"I'm guessing the best, right?"

He gave Bogi the sit command. The dog made himself at home but kept his ears up. "It has to be for obvious reasons."

"So you have this side hustle? I mean, contract work, because of your experience in the military?"

"Yeah, on an as-needed basis."

Isla studied the sparely decorated cabin. A nice fireplace, a galley kitchen with a two-burner stove and small refrigerator, and a lot of windows with the curtains drawn. A front door with heavy bolts, and a back door with a fancy security box attached to it. A safe house masquerading as a quaint cabin.

What had he gotten her into?

She sank down onto the worn plaid couch and tugged out her laptop and phone while he fed Bogi some food he'd dragged out of a closet and poured him some water. The dog lapped it up, then shook his head, the rivets on his collar shining.

"Okay Bogi, you deserve some playtime." Pulling a roped ball out of the same closet, he threw it toward the big dog.

Bogi leaped into the air to catch the toy, then retreated to a corner to enjoy gnawing on his treat.

Those two had a bond that she'd seen working for the K-9 team. Bogi and Michael would protect her, but mostly, they'd take care of each other, too. That brought her a small measure of comfort.

After Michael did another search for listening devices, and checked both their rucksacks for bugs, only to find nothing, she turned to him. "I need to let Chase know I'm okay. I only hope these people didn't go to my house." She pushed at her hair and tried not to panic. "What if they did?"

Glancing at the door, Isla wanted with all her being to run.

Michael stood in her way. "Isla, don't do anything to endanger them or yourself."

"I haven't. You have."

"I know and I'm going to fix it." He guided her back to the sofa, while she wished she hadn't been so sharp with him. But hey—stress.

"They don't know where you live. Yet."

He helped her sit down and then checked the curtains and blinds before pulling kindling from a woven basket to start a fire. "Send Chase a message but not on your phone. Send it on your fancy laptop."

"I can do that," she replied. Then she got to work, ignoring the cup of hot tea Michael brought to her.

I might be out of town for a while. Can you water the plants? Use the gold key. And make sure the house is secure since no one should be there now. Sorry—got tied up at the lab but I'm out now and with a friend.

Michael brought over a cup of instant coffee for himself and sat down beside her. "Mind if I read it before you send it?"

She pushed the laptop around and took a sip of the strong but slightly stale tea, shivers moving down her spine despite the fire burning away. Nervous and worried, she kept talking despite her brain telling her to shut down. "The gold key is code for I'm in trouble. My granny always had a safe word

for us to use if something happened. If…
my biological dad ever tried to find me."

Michael's eyes darkened, making her
wish she'd stayed as mysterious as he
seemed. This man would easily commit
murder to save Bogi and her. "Did he harm
you?"

She did a quick head shake, but the flood-
gate had been opened. "No. He died in
prison when I was twelve. He'd been put
there for domestic abuse, but he got out
after a few years. Then he was sent back
the second time—for murder. I didn't know
he'd died so Granny and I were always
careful. Even though we finally found out
he couldn't hurt me, we still used the code."
She inhaled a breath and let it out.

She took a breath then let it out, and the
pressure of her situation hit her full force.
"He went back after he killed my mother
when I was too young to understand. I
didn't know what had really happened until
I was older. Now, I like having information
firsthand." Frantic, she tried to gather her
thoughts. "I need to see the whole picture,
Michael. I'm not good at trusting people."

Michael shook his head, his eyes full of sympathy and anger, a jagged pain etched in his rugged features. "I'm sorry, and I mean that. I had no idea."

"I've never told anyone and I really don't know why I told you. I don't talk about it, you know."

"I understand, and I won't repeat what you've told me."

She believed him, but now he knew; now he'd seen her vulnerable side. "I imagine you have a thousand secrets inside that head of yours," she replied. "So I'll keep your secrets if you trust me with them, same as you keeping mine."

"That works," Michael finally said. "You've established you're safe and with a friend, but still in trouble. We'll wait to hear from Chase."

He went back over to the kitchen and pulled cans out of the top cabinet. "I have soup and soup."

"I guess I'll have soup," she replied, suddenly hungry. Nerves. She'd always been that way, eating when anxious, or not eating because she was worried. But she also loved exercising out in the open air and eating healthy food when she could, a delicate balance. Tonight, her world had tilted and gone off balance. So soup.

He heated the soup in a big mug and brought it over with a sleeve of crackers. "Vegetable beef and not-so-fresh crackers."

"I'll take it." She nibbled a cracker and took in a spoonful of the salty mush. "Thank you."

He ate his and then placed his bowl on the battered coffee table. "I'm sorry, Isla."

She studied him, wishing they could have gotten to know each other under normal circumstances. He was a good man, a handsome man, but one she'd kept on the back burner as a coworker and acquaintance, no matter that she got a bit flustered when being around him. But those times had been brief and all business, or at functions with their coworkers. Not like this, alone with him in a cabin that seemed to shrink each time he prowled around the room.

Finally, she spoke. "Yeah, me too, for so many things."

Then she sat up straight. "Tell me who

reached out to you to protect Bogi. We start there."

Michael ran a hand down his five-o'clock shadow. "My friend Dillon Sellers. He's moved up the ranks and is now a chief master sergeant at Lackland. He knows how I feel about Bogi. I had mentioned to him that I'd like to petition to take Bogi—adopt him—and retrain him, get rid of his trauma, give both of us time to heal." Michael looked away and then back to her. "I kept getting turned down, but now…"

"He got in touch with you after he realized Bogi had a target on his back?"

"Yes. After a big write-up in a local paper, the cartel got wind of it. The story made the national news, so word got out. And the bounty grew to a million dollars. I agreed on the condition that I'd be allowed to take Bogi. We got clearance to bring Bogi here. I've had him in an enclosed room at the clinic. I cleared my schedule and stopped kenneling any other animals over the holidays. I live right next to the clinic, and I have cameras on at all times."

"How long have you been hiding him?"

"About three weeks now." He shrugged. "I thought we were safe."

"Someone must have been aware, even before you picked up Bogi. The cartel must have hacked into your security system."

"Yes, and that's why I came to you. I think they definitely tapped into my security system and cameras. They could have been watching Bogi and me the whole time with eyes on the street and with monitoring the clinic and my home. Which is why I can't go back there either."

"What tipped you off?" she asked, her head in the game now. But her heart burned with worry for Granny and Enzo, which urged her forward.

"I heard a noise outside." He took the last sip of his coffee and shoved the mug away. "I went out the front door and saw a man running away. A man I thought I recognized."

"You think someone you know could be in on this?"

"Maybe. He's a local—Ralph Filmore— a retired veteran who hires out doing odd jobs. Someone could have hired him and sent him as a distraction so they could get to Bogi, but I scared him away before anything happened. Ralph is a good man, but his issues make him gullible. I've tried to help him, but he doesn't socialize well."

"They took advantage of that."

Michael let out a deep breath. "Yep. Which means they'd been watching for a while and had seen him coming and going. I knew we'd been compromised so I grabbed some things and got Bogi into my truck as fast as I could. And I came to you because I wanted to see if I could track down the whereabouts of my friend Dillon, and also find the cartel members who've scattered since that big raid. And possibly track some people from my past." He let out a grunt. "Like I said, I think my past has caught up with me. Someone wants Bogi badly, but someone also wants me."

"For reasons other than you having Bogi?"

"Yes, and I think the answers are hidden somewhere deep in the system."

Isla stood and whirled to stare down at him. "The military system?"

"Exactly. I think someone back in Texas is setting me up."

FOUR

Isla kept pacing until she had her heart rate under control. "We start with everyone you knew from this raid that went bad. If you and Bogi were involved and someone from your team is after you, what's in it for them? Revenge, the reward, anger, justice or a psychopath getting thrills?"

Michael stared up at her with a mixture of apprehension and pride. "I think you've covered every angle, and frankly, it could be any or all of the reasons you've mentioned. Or it could be the enemy seeking retribution. You seem to understand that kind of thing."

She placed her hands on the back of the couch and faced him. "I have to cover all the bases. It's what I do. Who in your past would have a grudge against you? And could they be working with this cartel that's after Bogi?"

"Well, there could be a long line," Michael said, his eyes distant. "It's war, you know. Things happen and people have to blame someone. But I hadn't connected the two, no."

"And?"

Michael's expression held tight to his secrets, a window closing with a hard click, silence shouting at her. He deflected. "You're good at this, aren't you? Not only the technical stuff, but at asking all the right questions, too."

"I've had a lot of hands-on training and I've been around police officers—on both sides of the law—most of my life."

He smiled, which made him even more intriguing. "On both sides? You mean you've been in trouble with the law at times?"

"When I was in the system, yes," she admitted, her own dark moments bubbling up while she fretted about Enzo. What would happen if she never made it home to him? Michael needed to understand her urgent need to be with the little boy.

"My mother was a police officer. After my biological father killed her, the whole department watched out for me so I always turned to the police when I was afraid or concerned. That's why I studied criminal justice and became a tech analyst. He was an abuser, and he did what they all do. If he couldn't have her, then no one would."

Michael stood and came around the couch and tugged her against his chest. "Again, I'm so sorry and as you said about me, I wished I'd known this before."

"I'm only telling you now because I want to go home to Enzo and my grandmother," she admitted, the panic she'd held at bay breaking through to wash over her. "It's hard to explain. My granny and my mother were estranged because of my father. My parents were never married, but they lived together. Granny only learned about me after years of trying to piece together what happened. She spent a lot of time and money on tracking me down. I'd aged out and had no idea where to go or what to do. She showed up one day and told me she loved me and offered me a home and a college education."

Pulling away, she wiped her eyes then focused on Michael. "Which is why I want to get back to her and Enzo and celebrate this special Christmas with the people I love. I have to get to Enzo."

Michael stood across from her, his gaze dark with understanding and regret, misty with memories and misery. He looked away and then back to her. "I will make that happen."

She took two steps back before she caved and tugged him close again, anger warring with hope. "I'm going to hold you to that. First, let's check your security system for bugs. Then let's figure things out from the beginning. Make me a list of names and I'll research those first. It could be that someone from your past got caught up in this cartel and now has to make amends."

"Isla?"

She ignored the way he'd said her name with a hint of a plea, but she'd told him too much already. She didn't want to bend or break, not now. "I'm okay, Michael. I want to get this over with, please."

Michael went to a drawer and found a pen and paper. "Then let's get started."

Michael watched as she did her thing, going through back doors on the dark web to check his system, her head down, her lips tight, the tail of her ponytail like a soft golden-brown wrap against her neck. Three in the morning, but she kept on going even after she'd revealed her darkest secrets to him. Her mother—a police officer—hadn't been able to save herself. Isla tried to save everyone to make up for that.

And now, she was reliving the nightmare of what could go wrong. They had to hurry.

"See anything?"

Isla's gaze glowed with determination as her fingers moved with ballerina grace across the keyboard. "Oh, yes. Someone definitely hacked into your system." She hit a few buttons. "We could scan your videos, but that might alert them. We know they hired a local to mess with you—a distraction—while they planned to get inside."

Tension filled Michael's body, a burn flaring inside his stomach. "I let my guard down."

"No, they went around the guard walls. It happens."

"Not to me," he said, knowing he'd become complacent. "Well, we can't go back and change that."

"No, but I can alert a colleague to get that bug out of your system."

"Okay."

"I've also sent out feelers on some of the names you submitted. We should hear back on those soon."

"Thank you." He wondered if some of his old team members still blamed him for the loss of life they'd caused that day. Most of them had stood by him, but he had made the call to go forward with the operation based on the intel they'd received. Dillon had stood by him, never once accusing or pointing the finger at Michael. So why did Michael still feel so guilty?

And why couldn't he get in touch with Dillon? Had someone already got to his friend? Twisting his head left and right to ease the tension, Michael knew he couldn't keep Isla on the run. He'd have to think of something, and quick.

She tapped a few keys and sent another encrypted message. "This goes to a private message board, and it has thick, strongly protected walls. If this doesn't work, I have an AA back in the city."

He nodded, even more impressed with her. "Thank you." An AA was an accommodation address—an old-school way of getting messages out to agents and assets, like a private mailbox, a cutout hidden from the world. It could be a facility or a go-between person. It made sense in her line of work. He'd keep that information close.

Isla watched the pings and dings on her laptop screen. "Hey, wait. I think Chase is reaching out."

That got his attention. Chase wouldn't be happy about this, but Michael could handle Chase's anger. "What does he say?"

She read the message:

Plants watered. House secure. No one is there now. Used the gold key. Checked for you in the lab. Saw you'd left with a friend. Busy at work now. Hope you have a safe trip. Keep me posted and say hello to your friend. I can't wait to hear the details.

"That sounds tight," Michael said. "He's moved your grandmother and Enzo. He's good, he's busy."

"He's investigating this," she added. "And us—why we're involved in that shooting. He might find the truth before we do."

"He doesn't know about the details behind me doing this job, so he won't know exactly where to look. We'll stick with you sending updates. I try to keep things vague."

"You don't have the luxury of being vague, Michael. I might not be there to tell him the caliber of the bullet that took down that man, but Chase already knows you fired the shot. He'll be all over trying to figure out why."

"You're right," Michael said. "I met Chase when I first arrived. Because he's

FBI, I had to read him in on my cover. He's a shrewd man and devoted to serving justice."

"Wait. You came here to work as a veterinarian, using that as a cover for your other work?"

"I did," he admitted. "But my other work is supposed to be few and far between. I might not be in special ops anymore, but I still have credentials and clearance in certain areas."

She glanced up, her chin down, and gave him a direct stare. "Like a ghost?"

"Something like that."

"But you were wounded. Does that bother you now?"

She was fishing for details so she could vet him even more than he'd already been checked. "A head injury and a lot of scans, X-rays and therapy. I'm okay now, but I couldn't go back out there and risk messing up another mission."

"Did your trauma mess up the last one?"

"No. I was okay when we raided that village. I took a bullet and hit my head going down. Hard. On cement."

"Ouch. I can see why that would stall things. TBI?"

"A bad case of traumatic brain injury, yes. I still get headaches when I'm tired, but I've been coping, leading the simple life, taking my meds."

"And now? How do you feel right now?" Her voice held concern coupled with anxiety. She still didn't trust him.

"I'm fine. Tired. Tense. But okay. You have to believe that, Isla."

Glancing at her watch, she said, "You should sleep."

"So should you. I can't sleep but I can stand watch."

Her laptop pinged. "Hold on." She studied the screen and then said, "So far we've found that one of your team members died of cancer last year. George Parton?"

"Yeah, a good man. We called him Dolly. Drove him nuts. We lost touch. He wouldn't have it in for me anyway."

"How about Tennessee Sanders? He's back in Tennessee and working as a security agent."

"Tenn Man? He's clean. I visit him now

and then. I could reach out to see if he's heard or seen anything."

"I'll keep him on the list." She moved over all the names associated with his team. "Dillon is here, of course. But then, you'd have no reason to suspect the man who asked you to protect Bogi, right?"

"Right." A tickle went down Michael's backbone.

"Michael?"

"We've had our moments, but Dillon is solid."

"Does he have a nickname?"

"Yes." Michael smiled. "Dill Pickle."

"That alone could make him want to get revenge."

Michael got serious again. "It's not him." He couldn't see Dillon holding a grudge. "We were given the wrong intel, but the responsibility fell on my shoulders. Dillon vouched for me through the whole investigation."

"Okay, then."

"You don't believe me?"

She stood and stretched like a sleek cat.

"I want to believe you, on finding your enemies and everything else. I've told you that. But you have to admit yanking me out of my comfort zone when I'd planned to go on vacation doesn't exactly make you one of my favorite people." She smiled.

"Was I ever one of your favorite people?" he asked, mainly to stall her and throw her off.

Surprise shifted to sarcasm in her eyes. "I liked you, but I didn't know you that well. Obviously. I still don't know you, but now I sure know *about* you. You're leading two lives and that is not an easy feat. I can barely deal with one life, so I don't think I'm quite ready to cope with your double identities."

He leaned against a chair and crossed his arms over his chest. Why was his pulse increasing with each second she stared back at him, her defiance moving from her eyes to her lifted chin?

He sent her a straightforward stare. "Would you like to get to know me?"

She let out a laugh and he grinned, glad

he could ease her worries for a moment. Then she pushed at her ponytail and let out a sigh. "I would like to get to know you because I'm the curious type and because I find it hard to trust people who aren't honest with me."

He sighed. "I guess I've blown the first-impression thing, haven't I?"

"Pretty much."

They both went silent. He, leaning on the chair—her, standing by the old leather desk chair. Bogi's gaze ping-ponged from one to the other, while they kept eyes on each other. The silence lapsed into something else. A pause that became palpable.

Michael moved toward her, only wanting to reassure her, make her feel safe. She stood, her dark eyes flaring.

Then they heard a crash outside and the moment was gone in a flash of movement. Bogi leaped into the air and snarled, clearly having his own moment, ready to fight.

Isla shut everything down and dropped her small laptop into the dark recesses of her big backpack. "On the run again."

Michael grabbed his weapons and tugged her around the old leather sofa. "You might have to leave that behind."

"I will not," she exclaimed. "I'll use it for a weapon before I let go of it. This is the only thing I salvaged tonight."

She held her pack tight, causing him to realize she must have had one like this, living in the system, and she'd moved it with her from each and every home she'd had to live in, even the bad ones. A group home, before she aged out. How she must have protected that pack that held most of her belongings. Her treasures. He'd had a pack like that when he was on tour. Treasures he could send back home, or someone could send back home, if something happened to him.

"You can hold on to it, Isla, unless things get too hot. I have to save you, not that backpack."

"I can save myself," she whispered as they heard a ruckus outside. "I know how to hide."

"Not from the people after us," he warned, his heart leaping like Bogi's body, a need to protect her overtaking him. "Not from them." He went into action, setting up ways to trip and trick their intruders and buy them some time. By the time he'd finished with wires and moving heavy furniture, she wondered how anyone could get into this place.

A ping hit the window and Michael shoved her down.

"Bullet," he said. "The windows are bulletproof, but they'll have us surrounded if we don't hurry. They could start a fire to draw us out or set off a bomb to blow this place apart."

Those scenarios weren't helping her anxiety at all.

"How will we escape?" she asked, her gaze scanning every window in the same way she scanned the codes moving across her computer screen.

"I have a plan."

"That makes me feel better," she said on a droll note. "Want to share?"

He pushed at the sofa and then pulled up the rug that had been underneath the sofa. "Yeah. A tunnel through a cave that leads to a road where there's a shed with my old Jeep inside it."

Something hit at the door. More bullets or a human?

"It's time to move," he said, grabbing his own gear.

He pushed the sofa toward the front door to stall them, then tugged at the heavy rug again, just enough to open the portal. "Ladies first."

Isla looked at him, then looked down into the dark tunnel.

"Here," he said, nudging her.

A flashlight. "Thank you. I don't like the dark."

"Neither do I." He pushed her down and then sent Bogi in with her and ordered him to guard. "I'm right behind you."

After securing the door, which pulled the rug with it when it shut, Michael reached where she stood hunched over and waiting. He slipped past her, the scent of her floral shampoo wafting after him, a garden he didn't have time to explore.

"Follow me," he said, a sadness covering

him in the darkness. She'd never follow him again after this, and they both knew that.

But this long night had to end one way or another.

Because dawn was coming.

FIVE

The tunnel held smoky lanterns lined up like mason jars full of fireflies, the silky shadows of spiderwebs and dust merging to give the walls a creepy, moldy glow. That didn't help Isla's anxieties or settle her nerves. She'd never liked dark, dank, closed-in places. Maybe because one of her foster moms had hidden her in closets when she'd acted out? Or had the same thing happened when her mother had hidden Isla from her father? Did babies remember such things?

"Hey, you okay back there?"

She blinked as Michael and Bogi rounded a curve that gradually began to elevate them. "I'm fine. Having a lovely Friday night—I mean Saturday morning—full of revelations and secrets. What's not to like?"

"So you're not fine?"

"I don't like any of this, but I especially don't like this tunnel and any minute now I'm going to have a panic attack if you don't get me out of here."

"We're there," he said, hitting on a button that opened what looked like a hatch out of some kind of dystopian movie. "Feel the cold air?"

She did, she felt the breath of fresh air hitting them. Bogi jumped out as if they were playing in the park, but he did a scent scan that showed this wasn't a park and he wasn't playing.

Michael helped her up the ladder and then tugged her to the left. "The Jeep's about a klick to the west."

A half mile or more, she figured while she studied the brutal terrain. "I can make that because I'm breathing again," she said, taking in a deep breath of the cold dawn air. "First that tiny cabin and then the tunnel. Our time together is nothing short of strange, Michael."

"Okay, got it. You're not happy, but we need to stay in the shadows and we have about ten minutes before the sun crests over that ridge to the east."

"Should we run?"

"No, but we can walk fast and stay crouched near the thickets and rocks, just in case."

"Got it." The man had gone from spy to soldier in a click of his own. How could she ever look at him in the same way after this? If they even got out of this.

They crouched and walked in a hurry until they reached an old shed, their breaths causing steam to lift out over the still, muted air. Michael opened the rickety locked door with a key from a big key chain inside his jacket, where she assumed he also had a change of clothes and some MREs—Meals Ready to Eat. James Bond or Jason Bourne? Or a desperate man trying to save a dog?

Bogi glanced at her as if he'd read her mind. Isla gave the dog her strongest frown but he didn't even flinch. Tough, that one. Exhausted and full of angst, she'd become giddy and a bit bold.

"Where to next—the Riviera?"

"I wish."

She had an image of him swimming in the sea, swimming toward where she sat on a lounge chair in the sun.

"Hey, stay with me."

She blinked again and got her thoughts back on track, back to the worry hole she'd carved in her brain and heart. She wouldn't cry, but bursting into tears would help her feelings. Only not so much her predicament. She couldn't run away now. She needed his protection. And…he needed her.

Another revelation that floored her. Michael needed her. And not just her expertise. He needed someone he could trust to get through this with him. Could she?

As he got them into the Jeep—*old* didn't begin to describe it—she thought of Enzo's dark eyes, so bright with hope, and Granny Annie, her one champion. Did they know how much she loved them?

"Are you going to make it?" Michael asked as he cranked the choking, coughing vehicle and geared it into a fast run along the bumpy mountain lane that would take them away from danger.

"I'm trying," she said, tears burning hot

in her weary eyes. She should be home right now, waking up to her new world with Granny and Enzo.

"We've lost them for now, but we don't have much time." He glanced at her, and he must have caught the look on her face because he said, "I can't do this to you anymore, Isla. I'm going to find a place where you can be safe with your family."

Isla burst into tears then. She couldn't speak so she didn't reply.

Bogi glanced at her again and this time he whimpered under his breath, his big, dark eyes full of understanding.

The same as Michael's gaze landing on her for a brief second before he turned to face the road ahead of them.

Once they were safely miles away and headed in a zigzag of back roads, the long way back to Elk Valley. Michael glanced over at her. "I've made up my mind. I'm going to find a place to stop and I'm going to give you a message to send to Chase. I don't want to use my cell phone. I'll need him to set up you and your family in another place, not exactly an official safe house. The people after us might know all of my hidey-holes, so this will be different but somewhere with protection and still nearby, so we can possibly work with Chase on this."

"What have you got in mind?" she asked, swiping her eyes, hopeful for the first time since he'd walked into her lab.

He pulled the old Jeep over onto a lookout surrounded by rocks and trees then backed it off the road to hide it a bit and have it ready to take off if needed, something she'd do in this situation, too.

"A ranch," he said. "A big one with a lot of people around to keep watch and a lot of gun power to back that up."

Isla listened, her laptop ready, while they checked the road several times. Wondering what Michael wanted to convey, she waited to type his message, exhaustion finishing off what little adrenaline she had left. Her eyelids felt like heavy spools of weight and her hands shook a little bit. She missed her home and the life waiting for her.

Michael did one more scan and then started:

Need to find a quiet place for my friend to be alone. MNFour should do the trick. It's secluded and has great views from every room. Can't wait to see the relatives there? I'll take care of the rest. Thx—Doc.

She looked up at him after she'd typed the words. "MNFour? As in the McNeal Four Ranch near Laramie Mountain?"

"The very one," he replied, his tone heavy with hope and regret. "It's secluded and Cade McNeal knows his way around guns and horses, which could both come in handy. Plus, he owes me a favor for saving one of his mares and her colt during a rough birth. And another plus—his wife, Ashley, is a K-9 officer."

"I know her," Isla said. "Obviously."

He lifted his chin, his dark gaze on Isla. "Obviously, which means you'll feel comfortable around her. She'll help protect you and your family."

"Is the ranch one of your safe houses?"

"Nope."

She wouldn't get anything more out of him on that point. So she tried again. "That's not a big ranch house."

"No. And they might not agree. But for now, I think it can work. You'll be safe and we can keep trying to protect Bogi from the people after him, whoever that might be."

She would love to stay with Ashley and Cade. Ashley had been a rookie cop with the Elk Valley PD when Isla had been recruited as a member of the team they'd put together to catch a serial killer. The MCK-9 Unit had become a family and had been commissioned to work together on other cases. But Isla didn't want to put anyone else in danger.

"Are you good with this?"

"Yes, as long as we can keep everyone safe," she replied. "Now while we wait, let's consider what we know so far."

"Not much," he said, "but I appreciate your hard work. We've ruled out several people from my past."

"The cartel sends out red flags," she replied, her mind spinning again. "But maybe that's too obvious. We know they have a bounty on Bogi, but we also know they have ways of getting to people that no one ever sees. Why send a lonely retired veteran, and one with issues at that, to distract you? They would have gone in with guns blazing and taken out both of you."

"You make a valid point," he said, his gaze taut and all-seeing because of the image she'd presented. "We still need to consider the cartel members because they do want Bogi gone, and we can keep working on the remaining list of people from my past to jar any memories."

"Or we can consider combining the two," she reminded him. "They could be working together to off both Bogi and you."

"Yes." He went silent on that one, which made her think he wasn't telling her everything about his past. "Maybe your hacker friends will come through."

"I didn't say I have hacker friends."

"You don't need to. We all know they offer their services in exchange for not going to jail. Assets, of course."

"Of course. We'll leave it at that."

He smiled. The man sure had a nice smile but he didn't quite know how to use it.

"I hope I'll hear more on that," she told him, getting back on point. "Once I'm settled in one spot and have time, I can dig a little deeper in figuring this out."

"I hope the McNeals will take us in," he replied as they got closer to town. "I'm letting Chase do the asking because I'm sure he'll take over once we get there."

"Us, we?" She pivoted on the seat, her heart bumping along with the ruts on the old road. "You're not planning on staying at the ranch, too, are you?"

He gave her a glance that told her this was nonnegotiable. "I plan to, yes."

"Why?"

"To watch over you and your family, and to be close so I can help you research this."

"I'll have Ashley to watch over me."

"I understand and I can come and go. I have to get back to my clinic and tidy things up but I'll be alert and careful. My receptionist has to be wondering where I am, though she's used to me having to leave town now and then without notice. I have a friend who fills in for me at times like this. I need to let her know, too."

Her.

His friend—a her. Well, none of Isla's concern, so why did hearing that rub against her skin like grit. A man like him would draw women like flies sticking to sugar. Quiet, a bit intimidating, mysterious and good-looking. The hard-to-read kind of man that made a woman want to get inside his head and figure him out, change him in places and keep him the same in other places. The wrong kind of man for Isla.

Or so she kept telling herself.

Her laptop dinged, causing her to break free of daydreaming. "Chase," she said.

Michael straightened in his seat. "Read it to me."

Your vacation is all set. Will pick up supplies tonight—and two suitcases. MNFour is booked. Should have some peace and quiet. Can check in ASAP. Will discuss future plans when I see you.

* * *

"We're in," Michael said, a long sigh of relief washing over him. "I feel better knowing you'll be with your family and safe again. I shouldn't have done this to you."

"It's okay." Her eyes burned a glistening bronze as the rising sun shimmered over the mountains off in the distance.

"No, it's not okay," he said. "I don't usually panic, but I had to think fast and get Bogi away from there. My mind went to logistics and analysis. I thought I could do this job alone and get intel then be on my way."

Isla watched the sunrise, her voice husky as she turned to glance at him. "I want to help you. I'm trying to do that. What's done is done, Michael. We'll get through this. I'm used to getting through things."

That comment hit Michael in the gut. He had a new perspective on the tech analyst, a new admiration for Isla. She worked hard and did so with purpose. She wanted justice in much the same way he did. She'd been through so much and yet, she rolled with the punches and recovered with a coolness that impressed him. But she shouldn't have to get through things.

"I'll make this right," he said.

Her laptop pinged again.

"Chase?"

She shook her head. "One of my contacts." Her gaze danced over the screen and then back to Michael. "Michael, the man you saw running away from your clinic last night…"

Michael's pulse quickened. "Ralph?"

"Yes." Isla swallowed and looked back at the screen. "Found dead in a ravine about a mile from your clinic."

Michael hit the dash, causing Bogi to jump to attention behind them. "They killed him. He's no longer useful so they killed him. This is what they do, Isla."

He cranked the Jeep and spun out.

Isla held on and gave him a quick glance. "Michael, be careful. I'm sorry about your friend but you need to stay on the alert. They want you to give them Bogi."

"I'm not going to cave. I'm going to find

the people doing this and I'm going to make them pay."

Isla shut down the laptop and held it against her stomach.

"I didn't mean to upset you," he finally told her. "I'm so angry and you're right. I need to control my temper. Anger got me into trouble the first time I made a mess on that mission. I won't let it ruin me again, and I especially won't let it ruin you and your life. That I can promise you."

Isla's eyes had deepened to a burnished brown in the morning sun. The touch of her hand on his sent a warmth throughout his system, giving him strength.

"I won't let that happen either," she said. "Not to you or to me. We'll figure this out together, Michael, because that's what we do, right?"

"Yes," he said. "It's our job, but now it's even more. It's personal. And it ends with me."

SIX

"So here's the plan," Michael told Isla after he'd calmed down. "We need to find a hotel room and stay there all day until dark."

Isla didn't like hearing that, but he made good sense and she wouldn't complain. It wouldn't matter if she did. "Yes, because we can't arrive at the ranch in broad daylight. So where will we find a safe place?"

He watched the road behind them. "I know of a small, out-of-the-way motel near Long Lake. We can hang out there until tonight. We need to let Chase know."

She nodded, so fatigued she couldn't even argue with him. She typed a quick message:

Will arrive around dinnertime. Going to hang out and rest for a bit and enjoy the views.

Michael gave her a nod after she read it to him. "Okay, you do need to rest."

"I have to admit, sleep sounds good right now."

He zoomed to the north and Long Lake. "You can sleep and I'll do some digging of my own."

"How?" she asked. "You said you can't risk using your phone."

"I'll grab a burner," he explained. "I know a place."

"Of course, you do. Why didn't you mention that last night?"

"Last night and up until now, in survival mode, I tried to keep you and Bogi alive. We should be safe using your fancy laptop, but I need to make these calls myself. None of the people I'm calling would talk to you and they'd track your phone right away and probably expose our whereabouts."

"Burner phone it is, then."

She closed the laptop and then closed her eyes, the bump-bump of the Jeep luring her to sleep. But her dreams were dark and full of dangerous people, black closets and screams. She could hear Enzo crying and Granny calling out to her. She couldn't breathe.

She woke with a scream and felt the Jeep accelerating.

"Hold on, Isla," Michael said. "Someone is following us."

This was her nightmare.

Being chased on a winding mountain road, fearing for her life, worrying for her family. What could she do?

She'd pray. Prayer had always gotten her through the worst, and Granny had taught her to pray deep and with meaning after so many years of short chaotic and choppy prayers.

She closed her eyes as the Jeep hugged a curve with rocks on one side and a deep ravine on the other.

Dear Lord, help us now in our time of need. Protect Michael and Bogi and me. Keep my family and my friends safe. Help us to escape these evil people. Give us strength and hope, Lord.

Michael touched her arm. "Hey, you okay?"

"I'm praying," she said as they whirled and bumped, the ravine so close she could see dust and rocks spewing out around the vehicle and falling into nothing but air.

"Good idea."

He gunned the Jeep as they approached a downhill curve, a black truck grinding its gears behind them. "These back roads are a mess and treacherous."

"Really? I hadn't noticed." Her head hurt, and the lack of food and sleep had caught up with her. She'd pulled all-nighters before, but not while she was running for her life with a man who both thrilled her and confused her.

What has happened to my safe, quiet Christmas holidays?

"Yes," Michael shouted. He hit his palm against the shredded leather of the steering wheel. "I had hoped that would happen."

"What? They disappeared?" She twisted to see the truck behind them slowing down.

"Nope. The brakes are running hot on the truck."

"Oh, well." Her heart slowed down at about the same time he slowed the Jeep. "So they can't come after us anymore. For now?"

"Not with hot brakes." He glanced behind them. "Won't do any good to call this in. By the time the authorities find the truck, which is no doubt stolen or unregistered, the people in it will be long gone."

She nodded and inhaled a deep breath, then let it out. "I don't understand how they keep finding us. My equipment is encrypted to the max and you haven't used your phone. We both checked for trackers."

He nodded. "I can't imagine they would have planted anything on you before this started in the possibility that I'd go to you for help, and I've checked my clothes. But either they did plant a tracker we can't find or they've got eyes everywhere and they're toying with us. We'll have to hurry and hide the Jeep somewhere, then walk to the motel."

She went through her backpack again, checking every pocket and every corner. "I have the same things in here I carry home with me every night. My phone and the one laptop that I can use until I get back to the lab, and a few personal items." She stopped, looked over at him, then shook her head.

"What?" he asked, his dark eyes burning.

"What if someone got into the lab while I wasn't there. A cleaning person or someone dressed like an officer?"

"That's possible," he said. "They tapped into my clinic's security system somehow. But why would they bug your lab?"

"Maybe the man who showed up came there to do that but he stumbled on both of us instead?"

"But they'd have no prior reason to bug the lab," he reminded her. "Unless they were trying to bug the entire police station because they know I come and go there a lot."

"All possibilities," she said.

"All possibilities," he repeated. "We need a safe place to get it all together."

"The ranch," she said. "They'll have internet, at least, and I can take it from there. But we have to be careful. We don't want anyone attacking the ranch because we're there."

"No, but right now it's close and it's the safest place I can think of."

"Then let's get to that motel," she replied, ready to fall across a bed.

Then her laptop pinged an alert, causing both of them to jump.

"It's from Chase," she said. Then she read it to Michael. "Meet me at the Chateau. Now."

The Elk Valley Chateau was where most of the task force members who'd come from various states had stayed while trying to find the Rocky Mountain Killer. Now a hotel, it had once been a Victorian home. After being renovated, the huge structure with wraparound porches still held a bit of old-fashioned charm.

Unless your boss had summoned you there knowing you were in danger from bad people. Then it became a concerning place.

"He's mad," Isla said, her tone flat and firm, her exhaustion just messy enough to make her want to scream if anyone approached her.

"He's trying to protect us," Michael shot back on a low growl. "Doing his job."

But in his heart, he knew Chase had to be aggravated with him for going against any type of protocol and taking the department's best tech analyst on the run. Chase might be FBI, but he'd do anything to protect the team members who'd worked so hard all year to crack a big case and solve several murders. Chase and Isla had grown close during that time. Chase fit the big-brother type perfectly. He'd vouched for her so she could adopt Enzo and he'd blame Michael if she lost that little boy.

"But why call us in? I thought we were going to the ranch."

"We'll find out when we get there," Michael replied, trying not to think ahead. "I'll get you to the ranch and I don't care if Chase disapproves."

"Is that it, then? You believe he's not on board with this idea?"

"I told you I don't know. You read his statement. Nothing there to tell."

Isla stared over at him. "Someone else needs sleep, too."

"I'm sorry," he said, agreeing. "I'm to blame for you being here, for Chase having to get involved, for your whole world crashing around you."

"Yes, that's true," she said, without skipping a beat. "But I could have tried harder to sneak away. I believe you, Michael. I want to help you, but I need to know Enzo and Granny are safe."

She wanted to help him.

That told Michael a lot about Isla. Generous and loyal, she'd do anything for a friend. Even a friend she didn't know that well, more of an acquaintance, really. Well, until yesterday, and now they were getting to know each other pretty quickly—both good and bad.

"Let's talk to Chase," he finally said. "I should have gone to him first, but the FBI never likes to get involved with CIA or Homeland Security. We all think we know best."

"But you work for the Department of Defense, right?" She stopped, took a breath.

"Wait? So you work for whoever needs you?"

"Yes."

"Are you an assassin?"

"No."

"You told me you do contract work. Is that even true?"

"That is true."

"But?"

"But I can't tell you anything else."

"No wonder several people are after you," she said, the ebb and flow of his ever-changing nocturnal life bringing out the frustration he heard in her words. "You've obviously made a lot of people mad."

"I'm beginning to wonder if they came after Bogi as a cover, but they really wanted me all the time." He didn't say it out loud, but why would his friend send the K-9 here when the base could have protected Bogi? He'd believed Dillon needed his help.

She didn't ask what that might be. They were too close to the chateau now. He pulled around back and parked the Jeep under the mushrooming cover of a giant oak tree, hoping that could hide them for the rest of the day.

"Are you ready?" he asked her. A dumb question.

"I'm not sure what to say," she replied.

When they got inside and headed toward the big conference room, which resembled a large dining room, Michael opened the door and let her go ahead of him. He gave Bogi a command to stay. The dog sat by the door, but his eyes were on the people across the room. The dog had bonded with Isla, same as Michael.

"Enzo," she screamed as she ran toward the toddler and her grandmother, who were sitting on a small sofa. "And Granny Annie."

Bogi's ears lifted, but he remained in position.

"You're here," her grandmother said as she pushed at her dark curls. "Are you all right?"

Enzo giggled and squirmed to get down from Annette's lap. The toddler's dark hair and big eyes matched Granny's, even though they weren't related. Her grandmother's gaze gleamed with tears of relief. "Isla, I've been so worried."

"I'm okay," Isla replied. Then she reached out her arms.

Michael watched as Isla hugged her grandmother and her son close, his fatigue and the sight of all of them together again making him as mushy as a teddy bear. He didn't do mushy, but he felt the same relief, and something in his tired, burned heart shifted and softened. Isla shot him a thankful glance, then closed her eyes for a brief moment.

Michael looked over to where Chase sat in a chair, watching the scene. Then Chase turned, his smile freezing into a hard gaze as it landed on Michael.

Before Michael could say anything, his friend got up and grabbed him by the collar, anger smoldering like coals in his eyes. "What were you thinking, going to Isla with this mess?"

Michael let out a grunt but didn't flinch. He had to stay cool for Isla's sake. "I had my reasons."

Chase lowered his voice, but his words drilled like a screw being twisted into wood. "Well, you'd better explain those reasons. The police chief who is on vacation in California is not happy with you right now. Nora is upset that one of the few officers working the late shift got shot trying to keep that man out of the lab. He'll survive, but he's on leave until he fully recovers."

"What about the culprit?" Michael asked. "Did you interrogate him."

"He's not going to talk," Chase replied. "He forced an orderly to unlock his handcuffs then knocked the orderly out. He escaped and we haven't located him yet."

"Probably dead for failing on the job," Michael said. Just like Ralph Filmore.

"Yes, probably." Chase stood back and gave Michael a thorough once-over. "Were you or Isla harmed?"

"No, but I had to get her out of there. I wasn't sure how many were coming for me."

"So you decided to take matters into your own hands."

Chase didn't need to remind him that he'd done that very thing in the past and messed up miserably.

"I'm sorry about that," Michael said, his eyes on Isla and her family. "I needed some concrete information. I thought I'd covered my tracks, but someone followed me there. Or, as Isla and I think, someone had already planned to be there. We think someone has been watching my place and the station." He glanced around, not ready to trust anyone right now. "They know I come and go, which made it easy for them to follow me."

"You think?" Chase shook his head. "Michael, you know the protocol."

"Yeah, but they got to me, Chase. I think they set this whole thing up—me watching out for Bogi."

That comment caused Chase to do a pivot and drag Michael away from Isla's celebration. "And why do you think that?"

"Because I believe they're after me, too," Michael said. "They must have been watching me for weeks, even months. They knew my routine, hacked into my security system, sent a homeless veteran as a decoy and killed him when he failed. And somehow, they've managed to track us, even though we've pretty much gone to ground."

"They won't find you now," Chase said. "I've set things up at the ranch but only for a few days. You'll need to keep moving, and Isla needs to be off this case."

"But she's helping me to build this case," Michael argued. "We need a couple of days to dig back into my past."

"Your past? Isn't the cartel behind this?"

"I thought so," Michael said, aware that Isla kept glancing toward them. But she couldn't leave her son. She wouldn't leave her son again. "Now, after we eliminated several people from my past, we think maybe the cartel is working with someone. Rico Saconni could be offering a bribe, a payoff, or they're threatening my former team members. I don't know. I can't abandon Bogi to go hunt them down. I needed intel and fast."

"So you got Isla involved, and at the worst time possible."

"Yes, and I regret that."

"You and me both," Chase said. "I'll give you three days at the ranch and then I'll personally take over protecting Isla, got it? She's in the middle of adopting that little boy."

They both looked over at Isla. She lifted Enzo up and walked toward them. "First, Chase, I'm fine. Second, I'm not happy about this but Michael needs our help—my help. I have to let my caseworker know what's going on or I could lose Enzo."

"You don't have to do this," Chase said. "We could get you back to the lab and put guards on you."

"And put the whole skeleton crew in danger," she replied. "Nope."

"So you'd rather go on the run again."

"I'm not going on the run. We'll be at the ranch with Ashley and her K-9 partner. I do need your protection because Michael can't stay there with us 24/7."

"Well, we can all agree on that," Chase replied.

While he stared at both of them as if he knew something besides danger had been brewing between them.

SEVEN

Isla could see Chase wasn't happy with them. She wasn't thrilled about what had happened either, but Michael did at least get her back here as he'd promised. Thanks to Chase summoning them, Michael had suggested the ranch and Chase had concurred. Hopefully they'd get past being mad at each other and get this situation under control.

They both wanted the best-case scenario, but she wanted to get on with this and end it.

"Are we going to stand here all day while you two try to outdo each other like gunfighters about to draw their weapons?" she asked. "Bogi and Michael are in danger."

"And so are you," Chase reminded her, his tone all business.

"Yes, and we can't change that now," she replied as she rocked back and forth and kept smelling Enzo's baby shampoo. He snuggled against her chest, his dark hair curling over her collarbone. Oh, how she loved him already. Always. And she'd do what needed to be done to keep him safe. "We know how this goes. We work the case, same as any other case."

Michael gave her an appreciative nod while Chase stared at the floor.

"We do need to come up with a solid plan," Chase finally said.

Granny rushed over. "Let me take him while you three work this out."

Isla hesitated. "I don't want him out of my sight."

"They have a room upstairs," Chase explained. "I've had them here since last night with a female officer blocking the door, the drapes closed and tight security around this whole place. And just so you know, no one has been near your house. Too close to headquarters, I believe."

"Thank you," Isla said, relieved. Kissing Enzo's forehead, she handed him over to her grandmother. "I'll be up soon, Granny. I need a shower and a long nap."

"I have clothes for all of us," Annette said. "I wasn't sure how long we'd be in hiding. And I'll order some food to be brought up."

"We move you to the ranch tonight," Chase explained. "But I called you back here so you could see your family. We can hide them somewhere else, if you'd rather, Isla."

"I want them with me," she said too quickly. "If that sounds selfish, I'm sorry. But I'm so afraid these people will come after them to get to us, so I'd feel better knowing they're close. That way we can get them to safety."

"Maybe," Michael said, a plea in his gaze.

"Are you thinking differently now?" she asked.

"I'm trying to think of the best way to protect you and them. That might mean splitting you up."

"I don't want to be split apart again."

"He's right," Chase added. "They've harassed you all night long, after all of your attempts to lose them."

Isla took Enzo back. "What should I tell the adoption agency? Have you talked to them?"

"They know you had an emergency and had to leave in a hurry. They know Enzo is safe with your grandmother."

"So we have some time." Her heart rending, she glanced from Chase to Granny. "Would you feel better with me, or somewhere safe with guards?"

Annette touched Isla's hoodie sleeve. "I want to be where you are, *dulce Niña*." She glanced at Enzo. "But we must think of the little one."

Isla blinked back tears. "I don't know what to do. I want to keep you both safe."

Michael ran a hand down his five-o'clock shadow. "I can't promise I'll be able to protect all of you, but Isla, if you want them with you at the ranch, I will do my best to watch out for you and your family."

Chase nodded to that. "You'll have us checking in, and Ashley and her K-9 partner know what they're doing. Cade can handle intruders, too. We'll set it up like a fortress."

Isla stopped and closed her eyes, asking God to show her the way. Could she keep them close and safe?

"How about this?" Michael said, glancing from her to Chase. "We get you all to the ranch and you can rest and recharge. Meantime, Chase and I can do our own recon and research. When you're rested, you can get back to digging into who might be after Bogi and me. If things seems okay in a few days, we can decide then whether to move you or not. All of you."

"We don't want to burden Ashley and Cade," Granny said. "But from what Chase has told us, they're willing to house us for a while."

Fatigue fell over Isla like a smothering hot blanket. She couldn't be any use to anyone until she'd had some food and sleep. With her son close by.

Michael steadied her while Annette lifted Enzo out of her arms again. The toddler started crying, but Granny distracted him with the promise of a book and a good nap.

"I'm okay," she said. "I'm used to pulling all-nighters."

"You're not okay," he replied. "I'm taking you upstairs. Chase and I have some things to discuss."

"Don't fight," she said, a weariness dragging her down. She'd never felt this tired before, but the stress of the last few months, and now this, almost brought her to her knees.

"We aren't going to fight," Chase replied. "But we do need to talk about strategy and I'll want an official report. Washington isn't too keen on this type of thing."

"Washington isn't too keen on me right now anyway," Michael said over his shoulder to Chase.

"What else is new?" came a quick reply from his friend.

"What's he talking about?" she asked Michael after they'd reached the second-floor suite where Granny had taken Enzo.

Michael turned her toward him, the door behind them. "I haven't always played by the rules, Isla."

"Really?" She giggled and shook her head, punch-drunk with sleep deprivation. "I would have never guessed that."

She made the mistake of looking into his eyes and felt as if she'd plunged off a mountain, about to fall into a deep, dark lake. No one had ever made her feel that way. She'd only been with Michael a full day and she'd come close to dying several times now, but the bond they'd formed seemed like a brand that marked them and sealed them together.

He stared back at her, a trace of his secrets moving with a flicker through those mysterious eyes. "I'm not who you think I am," he said. "I made a big mistake on that mission and we lost a couple of the team members. It's hard to get over something like that. I don't like playing by the rules anymore. But I can now see I'm vulnerable because I've become content, complacent and almost happy here as a veterinarian and helping with the K-9 officer dogs."

"And now?"

"Now, I've put you in danger. You're a good person, Isla. Remember that."

"And you're not?" she asked, seeing through the barriers he'd tried so hard to put up. "Do you want me to remember that, too?"

He drew back. "Remember that, first and foremost," he whispered. Then he opened the door and checked the room before he tugged her inside and shut the door on his way out.

Isla stood there, thankful for her son and her grandmother. She had been almost happy, too, until last night.

No matter how this ended, she and Michael would have this bond, this tug, this need to know each other. All of each other. Could that possibly make both of them both completely happy?

Isla woke with a start, her dreams dark and full of gunshots and screams, and her on the run calling out for Enzo.

"You're safe. It's okay. You're safe."

In her dream, Michael kept telling her she'd be safe. In reality, Granny stood near the bed, her hand holding Isla's with a grandmother-strong grip, the kind that sent warmth and unconditional love straight to Isla's heart.

She sat up, searching for the clock, grogginess and confusion burning like a fire inside her mind, a sheen of sweat popping out along her backbone. Nine in the morning. "Enzo?"

Granny pointed to the couch across from the bed where her son lay with pillows around him. "He's still asleep."

"Granny," Isla said, all of her emotions bubbling to the surface like a lab beaker full of chemicals running over. "I've messed up again."

"No, you have not," Granny said, sinking down beside her to take Isla in her arms. "You didn't do anything wrong, but your need for justice is still strong."

Isla held tight to the one person who'd fought for her, even when she hadn't known about her grandmother. Granny Annie, as Isla called her, was her anchor in the storm. She clung to that anchor now, thanking God for this spunky, courageous woman.

"Michael is a friend," she replied as she finally left go and looked over at Granny, then wiped at tears. "I couldn't abandon him, but I didn't know all of this would happen."

Granny pushed at her curly salt-and-pepper bob and shook her head, her dark eyes full of concern. "He is also a grown man who has seen and done things you weren't aware of. But then, that's the nature of this kind of work, *sí*?"

"*Sí,*" Isla replied, wondering if she could find something less dangerous to do with her life. "I love my work and Michael needs me. It's natural for me to dive right in. And I need to get back to work."

"Not yet," Granny said, a hint of frustration flaring in her no-nonsense stare. "Chase and Michael left together to see what they can find out about the man who got shot in your lab. I understand he is now presumed dead."

"I would think so."

Her *abuela* gave her a stare that stretched wide and deep, with eyes that could read Isla's very soul. "How close are you and Michael?"

Isla couldn't say much right now, maybe not ever, because she couldn't explain these feelings she'd developed for Michael since last night. Did spending hours with someone really bring out the best in them, or the worst? Used to finding the worst in people sooner or later, she had to tread lightly on this one.

Isla lowered her chin. "We're friends."

Her grandmother grunted, lifted her hands, then dropped them back onto her lap with a shrug. "I see more when I watch him glancing at you, and when I see you trying not to glance at him. So tell me the truth and let's discuss this."

"I've known him for a while since he comes and goes at the department as the K-9 veterinarian and we've all socialized together at times," Isla replied, trying to deflect because her feelings were so twisted right now. "So yes, we care about each other. He's good at his job and he has a love for the working dogs—our K-9s. I've talked to him at work in passing, but I didn't know much about him, really. He came to me for intel that only I could provide."

"I have prayed for you all night and day," Granny said. "I think the adrenaline of this situation has brought you and Michael close. But that might not last once this is over."

When Isla didn't speak, her grandmother lifted her chin, forcing Isla to look her in the eye. "Or can it?"

Isla couldn't hide anything from Granny Annie. "I don't know," she replied. "I will tell you this. Michael needs me, and yes, we've become close. When this is over, he might move on. Or I may decide to change careers. Who can predict that?"

"And if you both stay right here?"

"Then we'll still be friends and we'll see where that takes us. Enzo is my first priority right now."

Granny nodded, satisfied for a while at least. "You'll eat," she said. Then she stood and pulled over a cart full of sandwiches and fruit, a water carafe and a thermal coffeepot, with oatmeal cookies on the side. "Where do you want to start?"

"I'll have a huge cup of coffee and a cookie," Isla said, her love for sweets nagging at her empty stomach. "Then I might eat a sandwich half."

"Okay," Granny replied. "But drink some water, too. You need to stay hydrated."

"Yes, *Abuela*." Hydration was the least of

her worries right now, but a grandmother was a grandmother, no matter the situation. Somehow, that brought Isla a huge amount of comfort.

They both smiled at that. Then Isla heard a giggle and saw her son's sweet little head peeking out from behind a fluffy pillow. "I think someone else might be hungry, too."

Enzo grinned and pointed his finger at her. "Mama."

For a brief moment, the world around Isla melted away and her life seemed almost normal again.

But she knew as soon as the sun went down, she'd have to make another move. And this time, she'd have her family with her. Would she save them from harm, or put them in danger?

EIGHT

Tension danced throughout Michael's body with a fast-paced beat that ticked right along with his universal military watch. The sun disappeared and several undercover vehicles lined the street, discreetly yards apart, but ready for business.

They'd take Isla and her family out the back way and get them into a dark van. Then their detail SUVs would lead and follow behind as they circled town and took a zigzagged path to the McNeal Ranch, where Ashley and Cade, along with Ashley's black lab K-9, Ozzy, would be waiting to take over.

Snow covered the night, but the roads were clear for now. According to the latest reports, the weather would soon change due to heavy snow predicted for the next few days, which could be good or bad. They could be snowed in, thus keeping any intruders unable to get to them, or they could become trapped by intruders who'd do anything to get to them.

Not a great scenario either but at least Isla, Enzo and Annette would be surrounded by people who were used to doing their jobs in any kind of weather. Protectors.

He used to be a protector, then he'd turned rogue and become something he didn't even want to think about. A machine that moved only to take down the enemy. That had worked until he'd hurt and killed innocent people based on the wrong intel. But he couldn't prove who had given him the wrong information, so he'd taken the fall for the team. Would it be the same situation now, all these years later? He'd vowed after that mistake to always have the best information before he made a move, to trust the people he needed to trust or else. But once again, he knew in his gut someone had fed him incorrect details to throw him off. He'd gone slack, enjoying his work at the clinic, being normal.

Nothing about this situation was normal.

And now, he'd messed up by getting innocent people involved again. This time, he wouldn't take the fall and he wouldn't do the dirty work. This time he'd be the one to track *them* down and do what needed to be done.

The right way.

"All set," Chase said over the radio when Michael's watch hit exactly 18:00. "Roads are clear and we've made sure we're not bugged or being watched. You ready?"

"Ready," he replied. "I'll go collect the cargo."

"Roger. Help will be waiting."

Michael knocked on the door to the suite where Isla and her family had been all day. He hadn't spoken to her in a few hours, when he'd stood at this door with her. A moment that he'd never forget for so many reasons. One being his attraction to Isla. He couldn't be attracted to her. Not now, maybe not ever. He put people in danger even when he tried so hard to keep a low profile and keep his nose to the ground.

Chase had interrogated him about what had happened, pulling out details regarding the last few hours, but when it came to the personal stuff, Michael had shut that down.

"What's the deal with you and Isla?"

"What do you mean?"

"I know those kind of looks between a man and a woman."

"You're in love now, so you're imagining things."

"Don't insult me, Michael. Isla is in a delicate place right now and you getting her caught in this mess isn't helping. Don't do anything you'll regret."

"Maybe you mean don't do anything *you'd* regret, Chase. I thought you trusted me."

"I do, but Isla is special. She had a tough life until her maternal grandmother came along. Now she's about to finally have the life she's dreamed of, adopting a kid and loving him so he won't have to go through what she went through."

"I know that. I understand that. I know what I need to do."

"That's what I'm concerned about,"

Chase had replied. "Now is not the time to go rogue, Michael."

"A little late for that," he'd responded.

He'd already done some of the recon work while he was out today. After going over every inch of the clinic with a keen eye, he'd found nothing to clue him in, so he'd shut it down, glad he didn't have any patients kenneled there right now. Then he'd called his assistant from a secure phone Chase had cleared for him and told her to take the week off with pay. Later, he'd circled around town and gone to the motel where he'd planned to hide Isla and left a few traces in a room he'd rented for the night.

He'd explained to Chase, "We can put surveillance on the Lookout Motel and see if they show up there. Then I'll have certain proof they've got me bugged somehow, or they have someone who's good at the job of tailing me."

"I'll send an undercover to watch," Chase said, after a couple of grunts. "You shouldn't be taking risks like that right now."

"I have to take risks to get this done, Chase." Then he'd looked his friend in the eye. "But I can promise you this. I'll go by the book this time. I won't get impulsive. I'll have solid proof when I bring these people down."

"And you'll abide by the law?"

"Yes. I will. I have to for Isla's sake."

Chase's grunts turned into a sigh of acceptance. "I'm counting on that, Michael."

Now it was showtime.

Chase came on the radio again. "Your instincts were spot-on. The Lookout Motel had a break-in in room 202."

Michael's heart dropped. "The room I booked this morning."

"Yep." Chase inhaled a breath. "We captured the intruder and he's in custody now."

"Just one?"

"Yep. On foot. Found an abandoned vehicle two blocks over with a stolen tag. The techs are dusting it for prints and anything else they can find."

"Is he talking?"

"No. Not yet. He's fidgety and says we'll regret messing with him. Let's get this deed done and we'll see if we can shake something out of him later."

"We can't have them following us or attacking us tonight. I have to get Isla's family to safety."

"I'm bringing out the cavalry," Chase replied. "I've talked on the phone with Isla, so she knows security will be tight. I've got patrols everywhere. We need to get started."

Michael wished he could have talked to Isla, but he'd decided to give her some space. He needed that, too.

"I'm on it."

After ending the call, Michael nodded to the patrolman on guard near the door. The officer let him in.

"We're ready," he said when he saw Isla turning to face him.

He inhaled a breath of air. She'd changed into dark leggings and a long beige sweater with a big turtleneck collar. She wore sturdy brown lace-up boots. Her bronze-colored hair hung in loose coils around her shoulders. She should be in a fashion catalog instead of sneaking around in the night with him.

"For the weather," she explained because he couldn't stop staring at her, and because she kept staring back at him, her dark eyes wide with questions. And something he couldn't read right now.

He cleared his throat and glanced away. "Good. I mean—that's a good idea."

Annette gave him a look that said *Back off*, and she did it with a smile that didn't quite reach her stern eyes.

Michael peeled his gaze away from the women. "Okay, let's get you two and Enzo out of here."

He grabbed their duffel bags and the diaper bag, noticing Isla had her beat-up leather backpack tossed over her quilted black coat. After he'd put their things in the SUV, he turned to see Enzo reaching out to him.

Michael glanced from the boy to Isla. "May I?"

She nodded as she handed her son over to him. For a moment, Enzo was caught between them. The little boy grinned up at Michael, then touched a chubby finger to Michael's face.

Isla gazed at Michael, something sweet and intense moving between them. He'd die for them if he had to.

The moment ended, but he sure hoped whatever she had in that bag of tricks would help them get out of this situation. They couldn't keep moving from pillar to post forever.

Or at least, she couldn't. He, on the other hand, could draw these people out and bring them to justice. That thought uppermost in his head, he hustled them to the waiting vehicle, marked as a cleaning van. Getting them quickly inside and settled, he hopped in the front passenger seat and did a scan of the area. Nothing. Nobody. Very few cars nearby and they'd all been checked and cleared.

"We're good to go," he said, earbuds transmitting the message on a secure line.

Nodding to the driver, he turned to check on the passengers. Granny sat in the far back with a female officer, while Isla and Enzo were in the captain seats, Enzo in a sturdy car seat and Isla buckled in.

"Everyone okay?" he asked, glancing at Isla.

"We're fine," she replied, her tone low and quiet.

He gave her a quick okay, then said, "We have a lead vehicle up front, and another one following. We've cleared everything—watching for any activities or anyone who might try following us. So far, we're clear."

Isla gave him a smile he could only see as the streetlight glided by. Her tense smile that told him she didn't really feel all that safe with him. He hated that. He wanted to protect her and the child and her grandmother. He wanted them safe.

They were a tight-knit little family.

His heart pierced with a deep longing, but he'd given up on a family a long time ago. Pushing that and the way she'd looked him in the eye earlier to the back of his brain, he focused on the mission.

Because he couldn't guarantee anyone's safety, really.

Even when he'd promised Isla that with every breath.

Isla kept glancing around, checking on Granny and Enzo. Relieved to have them with her, she prayed they'd all made the right decision by sticking together. She couldn't imagine them off somewhere with strangers, scared and worried.

But she didn't want to think about any harm coming to them if they were with her either. She'd be diligent in protecting them, and her instincts told her Michael would do the same.

The ranch sat several miles from Elk Valley, and about fifteen minutes from Elk Valley Park, located on the foothills of the Laramie Mountains. She'd never been to the ranch, but she'd heard Ashley talking about it several times.

She reached across and took Enzo's little hand in hers. The toddler giggled and kicked his legs, the tiny leather booties he wore knocking against the seat.

We'll be safe, she told herself. *We have to be okay.*

Ashley was a good officer, and Ozzy was a well-trained K-9. She didn't know Cade that well, but Ashley loved him so that counted in Isla's book.

Now she waffled between praying and hoping everything would work out. Chase had informed her earlier that he'd started his own investigation with the absent police chief's go-ahead, and Isla could add to the equation by pulling up phone records, bank account transfers and travel details on several people who might be involved in this. Michael wanted to dig deep into the whereabouts of the cartel boss, Rico Saconni— who had originally put out a hit on Bogi. He was still a suspect. Isla had suggested early on that Saconni and the cartel could be working with someone from his past. Now that seemed to be the case.

Possible cartel connections inside the government or the military.

That would make her work even harder, but she could focus on finding the truth so her family and Michael and Bogi would be safe.

She glanced out the window, the streetlights fading away as they drove through roads carved into the mountain toward another valley. Ranch land miles outside town. Isla rarely ventured this far out since she worked so much, but she had hiked in Elk Valley Park a few times with friends. She knew those trails, at least. Doubting she'd be able to leave the ranch house, let alone hike, Isla took in a breath.

Michael glanced back at her, his expression as stony and stoic as the mountains around them. She usually could read people, but not this one. Not this man who'd disrupted her life and dragged her out on the run with him. And yet, she knew he had a good heart underneath that rock-solid exterior. He was a believer, maybe one who'd lost his way. She could see that at least in the way he protected people and spoke of God. She'd caught him with his head down and his eyes closed a couple of times.

Had he been praying? She sure hoped so.

"How you doing?" he asked, looking back at her again.

"Nervous, worried, but safe for now," she admitted. "And so glad I have my family with me."

"We'll be there soon and you'll feel even better. Ashley is cooking chili and has hot dogs for Enzo."

"That's good. His favorite." Isla wasn't sure she could eat anything. "I'm thankful for Ashley and Cade."

"Yeah, me too."

He turned back to the front, his head moving back and forth while he checked the road and scanned the few vehicles driving it. From what she could tell by turning to face her grandmother now and then, no one tailed them.

Michael saw her glancing back and nodded.

Isla suddenly wanted to know more about Michael. She had the resources to find what she needed to know about him and she'd use those resources to help him and also get the truth about what had happened on the last mission that had sent him into hiding.

He'd kept fighting the good fight as some sort of spy and as he'd said—a machine. Punishment? Or redemption?

He was a confused human being who needed people in life, people he could trust and…and love. Whatever she found out, she had to trust Michael right now. What else could she do?

NINE

Michael went back over the protocol.

"Guards 24/7 around the perimeters of the ranch. I'll stay here tonight and check back in during the next few days. But no one else other than people who've been cleared can enter the house or the grounds. Understood?"

Cade and Ashley both nodded. "Understood," Ashley said, Ozzy by her side. The black Lab looked like a lovable lump of fur, but he would go to work in a New York minute.

"I've got a couple of hands watching out for things, too," Cade added, nodding at Michael. Then he glanced at Isla and Enzo. "You'll be as safe here as you would in some isolated safe house. My wife is a pro."

Ashley laughed at that. "Why, thank you, handsome."

Michael could see the love between the two of them. He looked at Isla and her eyes met his briefly before she lowered her head to kiss her son. The sight of them together tore through his gut like a fish-knife, jagged and painful.

He'd never thought of family before, but now this family stood front and center in his mind.

Getting back on task, he went on, "Okay, so now that we're all here and settled in, we can wait to hear from Chase on what he's found out. He's got feelers out on this situation. Meantime, Isla and I will do some online sleuthing and hope we hit pay dirt."

"How about supper first?" Ashley asked, getting up to move to the stove where a huge pot bubbled, the spicy smell of homemade chili wafting through the air. "You both need nourishment."

"I could eat," Michael said. "How about you?"

Isla's smile showed the strain of the situation. "I do like a good bowl of chili."

"And we have the hot dogs ready to cut up for Enzo," Ashley said, her grin making Enzo laugh. "I also have peas and carrots that I chopped up and cooked for him. Cade gets credit for the chili."

"Thank you," Isla said, giving them a smile. "I appreciate you doing this for us."

"We owe both of you," Cade said. "Michael is the best veterinarian in Wyoming. And, Isla, you helped me find my sister."

"I was doing my job," Isla said, clearly not wanting to take the compliment. "But I'm glad I could help."

"And we're glad we can do the same," Ashley said. "It's my job, but you're also my friend. So let's try to enjoy this meal and then you and Annette and Enzo can settle into the big bedroom we showed you down the hall. It's perfect since it's the main guest room." Glancing at Michael, she added, "We have a small office I carved out of the corner of the living room. You can have privacy there. Ozzy and I will keep watch across the room on the old couch, until Cade takes over around daylight."

"She's rearranging a few things and making the place a bit spiffier," Cade explained as he got them all to the table and passed the bowls full of chili. "I'm not that good with decorating a house."

"It's our *home* now," Ashley replied, smiling at him.

"It is that—now." He smiled back.

Michael felt the discomfort of watching two people in love while his own heart beat a strange flutter each time he looked at Isla. Crazy since they'd only been around each other for over a day or so. But maybe he'd known the good in her all along. Maybe he'd gone to her because he knew without speaking it that she'd be the one he could trust.

Chase has asked him why he didn't let him know this. "I could have taken you in and helped you. Isla didn't have to be involved. And don't give me that lame excuse about needing technical intel that only she could give you. You have contacts all over the planet."

Michael didn't have a good answer to that statement. He couldn't tell Chase he thought this might be an inside job. He'd speculated that, yes, but to put Chase off the trail, he hadn't confided in him all the way. Chase had agreed that Isla was the best at getting onto the dark web and getting into websites through back doors.

For now, his cover and Isla were safe. Thankful that Chase had put himself in the middle of this, Michael accepted that he couldn't do it alone. He needed to remember God was the one in control here, not him.

He'd prayed last night. Real prayers. Not just the brief choppy requests he'd carried around in his head. His faith had become stronger since he'd moved here because Chief Nora Quan and FBI SAC Chase Rawlston considered their strong faith as part of their shields. It protected them through good or bad.

He'd begun to lean on that again, even if he didn't think he deserved God's grace.

"How's the food?" Cade asked, studying him with an intense expression. "Giving you heartburn already?"

"No, it's good," Michael said, shoving

more of the steaming, spicy taco soup into his mouth. "The corn bread is amazing."

Isla grinned and bobbed her head. "I guess I was hungry after all. Or maybe it's knowing that I don't have to go on any more wild rides in Michael's Jeep."

"You don't like old Bessy?" he asked with a mock frown.

"*Old* is a good word for Bessy," she retorted. "I'm sore all over from the bumps and whiplash."

"She got us this far," he replied, his tone fun while the look he gave her had to be shouting his feelings.

"That's true," Isla said, growing somber. "You kept me alive and I appreciate that."

Michael wished they weren't sitting here in hiding. He shot a glance at her again and something flared like a firecracker between them. He saw so much there in her pretty eyes.

Cade cleared his throat. "More corn bread, anyone?"

Michael glanced around and then back to Isla, mortified.

From the interested expressions on their

faces, everyone else sitting at this table had also seen that flare of awareness sizzling between Isla and him.

Two hours later, Isla and Michael were cloistered over her laptop in the far corner where a small desk and chair had been set up behind a partial folding screen. *Cozy,* she thought while her finger typed away. *Too cozy.*

Michael leaned over her, watching the screen. The fresh outdoors scent surrounding him made her very aware of him and caused her to miss keys and hit the wrong buttons. He'd taken a shower earlier and smelled like fresh snow on cedar.

And they were alone in this tiny corner of the now-quiet house.

True to her word, Ashley sat on the couch on the other side of the room, pretending to read a book. But Isla had peeked around the screen a couple of times and had seen her friend near the windows or checking the doors, Ozzy by her side. Ashley had discreetly left them alone so they could get on with their quest. And this had become a quest. Like going through a round of a fantasy game maze on a lonely Saturday night.

Isla sighed and kept working, trying to find out more on Rico Saconni. What else could she do? Enzo and Granny were asleep in the big bedroom, him in a crib borrowed from Cade's sister and Granny in the queen bed she'd share with Isla. A female patrol officer sat guarding their door.

"So other than pictures of him with beautiful women hanging off his arms, Rico Saconni is hard to track down. But after breaking through some back doors and calling in some favors from some of my hacker assets, I finally found this." She stopped and downloaded a file, then pulled it up so he could see it. "RSC Trust."

"And what's that?" Michael asked, his gaze scanning the spreadsheet. "I'm afraid I already know."

"Well, after pushing through layers of companies, I found the owner of all of these *wrapped* companies."

"A company behind a company behind a company." Michael let out a sigh. "Saconni?"

"The Saconni family, yes." She pointed to some figures on the sheet. "Rico is the son of Ricardo, who is deceased. But Junior likes the good life and he owes a lot of money to a lot of people."

Michael glanced over at her. "Yes, a source told me after the big bust, Rico has let the family firm turn into a mess, even more trafficking of drugs, guns and humans, but not in the controlled and protected way his father did. Yet nobody can capture him or pin anything on him, and somehow the money keeps rolling in."

"And he keeps rolling it right back out. A gambling problem, too many cars and homes across the continents, and probably payoffs to a lot of women he's loved and left."

Michael nodded at that. "So what else do we have?"

"He's got all these shell companies lined up right here in Wyoming," she explained. "He's taking advantage of tax breaks and a lack of oversight that would control secret finances. And I'm guessing the drugs Bogi found would have been funneled through our great state because of all the LLCs his lawyers here have set up to hide and launder dirty money."

"A *Cowboy Cocktail*," Michael said. "Secret arrangements too good to resist."

"Yes," she replied. "Exactly."

"So a connection here means it would be easy for them to know about me, but how and who would have given them information?"

"They set these things up with independent managers and financial advisors," she said. "Do you know anyone who works as such?"

"No," he said, "I can't think of anyone but I'll see what I can add to this. Let's keep looking at the list I gave you—see where these people are now and what they're doing."

Isla planned to track both Michael and Bogi, too, from the time they'd been partners until now. She might notice something he'd skim right over.

When he went quiet she noticed his expression changing, going blank, a frown forming. "Do you remember something?"

"No, just a tickle. Kind of like I used to get when we were about to complete a mission. Like the missing piece of a puzzle that snaps into place at the last minute."

"We need that piece right now," she said, hoping he'd remember. "Let me know if you get it figured out."

He shrugged and rubbed a hand through his hair. "I still get memory lapses from my injury years ago. So this could mean nothing. Or it could mean that someone on the outside is working with the Saconni family, and if I can find the missing piece, I can find out who that is."

"This does prove that whoever is behind this has ties right here in Wyoming."

"And probably homes and legitimate businesses covering their crimes," he replied. Then he rubbed his forehead. "Now this will nag me until I figure it out. It's a start, so let's keep at it."

Isla didn't push him to remember. Fatigue etched his face and gave him a craggy, stone silhouette. He would work through this, she hoped.

"If we connect the two, we might find out

who's after Bogi and you, and more important, the motive behind it—something that
can stand up in a courtroom. They want
Bogi gone so he can't track illegal drugs
anymore. But why do they want you dead,
Michael?"

"That is the million-dollar question, isn't
it?" he replied, his tone low and grim. "And
that is the missing piece of the puzzle in all
of this."

"Yes." Isla yawned, then put her hand
over her mouth. "I'm sorry."

He pulled her out of the chair. "Don't
apologize. It's past midnight. Let me es-
cort you to your room."

Her heart did a fast pump as his strong
hands held her arms. To counter that, she
swallowed and said, "It's like…right there
down the hallway, Michael."

"I'm walking with you." He turned to
where Ashley sat. "Why don't you go to
bed and Bogi and I will take the couch."

Ashley nodded and gave them a sleepy
grin. "Ozzy can help Officer Mira guard
the back of the house."

Michael waited until Ashley got to her

room. "Get some sleep. You've uncovered a lot of good information. I was thinking of Saconni from a distance, but if he has ties right here in the state we have an even bigger problem."

"Yes, because this explains how they keep finding us. Someone local—someone we trust—could be leading them to us."

"Exactly." He still had one hand on her arm when they reached the door. Mira, an officer guarding the house, greeted them. "All's quiet in there and nothing much happening on this side of the house."

Michael motioned to the comfortable chair Mira sat in. "Take a break, Mira. I'll roam the hallway for few minutes."

Mira took off to the front of the house. "I'll be right back."

Isla almost giggled. "You are one smooth operator."

"Comes with the territory."

She poked a finger against his solid chest. "One day, I'm going to dig deep into who you are, behind all that intriguing spy-shield stuff."

He grabbed her hand and held it tight,

his eyes flaring with a heat that seemed to spark right down her backbone. "Careful. You might not like what you find."

Then he stepped back and gave her a soft smile. "Sleep."

Unlikely, she thought as she watched him stalk back up the hallway, her heart racing after him.

TEN

Ashley was in the kitchen the next morning when Isla got up, the smell of coffee and bacon enticing and wonderful. She'd slept all night, but her dreams were full of distorted faces and dark alleyways, a sense of being chased hanging over her sleep.

"Hi," she said, pushing at her hair. "Where's everyone?"

Ashley handed her a cup of coffee and motioned to the table where bacon, eggs and biscuits were ready. "Cade is taking care of the animals and checking in with the guards. Mira went home, but I'll be here with you and we have patrols all around. They're searching the grounds and will be back in soon."

Isla sipped the strong coffee for fortitude,

and trying to be casual, asked, "And Michael?"

"I wondered when you'd get to him," Ashley said, her eyes as bright as spotlights that shouted, *Tell me everything.* "He said he had some business to attend to—following up on some of the intel you discovered last night."

Isla worried about Michael out there alone, but she had to remind herself this man knew how to take care of things. Or at least he'd done so up until now.

"Well, he's not safe out there." She nibbled on some bacon and glanced over to where Bogi lay with Ozzy. The big dog lifted his snout but didn't move. "And he left his K-9 here."

"For you," Ashley replied as she leaned against the counter and sipped a cup of tea. "Eat up before it gets cold. How are Annette and Enzo?"

"Still sleeping," Isla replied, noticing Ashley wasn't eating with her. "They're both worn-out."

Ashley looked at the food, set her cup down and then bolted. "I'll be right back."

Surprised, Isla watched as her friend headed into the bathroom. Ozzy stood, a worried expression on his dog face.

Isla tried to eat, but between worrying about Michael and wondering if he'd ever come back, and trying to figure out what was wrong with her friend, she could only take a few bites.

Granny came walking up the hallway. "I need a biscuit."

When she saw Isla stand, she waved her hand. "He's still asleep so enjoy this quiet time."

"I want time with him," Isla replied, about to head to the bedroom to watch Enzo sleep.

But Ashley rushed out of the bathroom, her face pale. "I'm sorry," she said as she hurried back into the kitchen.

Isla turned around. "Are you all right?"

"I'm fine," Ashley said, blushing.

Annette's gaze settled over Ashley and she let out a gasp. *"Ella esta embarazada?"*

Isla gave her friend a second glance after hearing that declaration. "Are you expecting?"

Shocked, Ashley held a hand to her stomach, then with tears in her eyes, started bobbing her head. "We found out last week. I wasn't going to say anything."

"You glow," Granny said, a soft smile on her face. *"Bonita."*

"She's right," Isla said. "You look beautiful. I'm so happy for you." She hugged Ashley. "But this means we need to leave and soon."

"Why would you want to do that?" Ashley asked, sinking onto a chair. "I'm capable of taking care of things. My sister-in-law and nephew, Melissa and Danny, are visiting friends, so I need some company."

"I know you're capable," Isla replied, remembering Cade's sister and her young son. "But Cade would never forgive us if something happened to you or the baby."

Ashley laughed and waved away Isla's worries. "I'm having morning sickness but I can still do my job."

Ashley stood, but Granny ordered her back down. "I'll make you some tea and you can nibble on some soda crackers."

Ashley nodded. "I hope this won't last too

long." She put a hand to her mouth. "I'm sorry, Isla. You're adopting and here I sit talking about morning sickness."

"It's okay," Isla replied. "I might not have a husband but Enzo will be my son—if I can get through this."

"Michael might have other ideas after you get through this," Ashley teased. "The man is smitten."

"*Sí,*" her grandmother said from the stove. "I'm not sure how I feel about that."

Embarrassment did a heated path over Isla's face. "Michael is a mysterious man who has a target on his back and he's try-ing to save a K-9 because he has a strong sense of duty. He is not interested in me right now, nor will he be later."

"Are you interested in him?" Ashley asked. "Please spill. This is keeping my mind off of being sick again."

"There is nothing to spill," Isla said, shak-ing her head. She didn't like the scrutiny or the questions. "We barely know each other."

"We think there is lots to tell." Granny handed Ashley tea and crackers. "You don't need to have feelings for a *desperado, chica*."

Cade and Michael came into the room and glanced at the surprised women. Cade laughed. "When you walk into a kitchen full of women staring at you with too much interest, you'd best walk away, buddy."

Michael grunted. "Oh, no. I want to know what they've been discussing here."

His gaze washed over Isla but before she could absorb it, one of Cade's hired hands came in. "Breach in the west pasture, Mr. McNeal. Two motorcycle riders, wearing all black."

Everyone went into action. Ashley forgot her tea and crackers and called out to Ozzy, "Guard."

The big Lab rushed to her side.

Michael alerted Bogi. "Stay. Guard."

"Take them to the back of the house," he told Ashley. "This could be another distraction, but we need to check it out." Then he turned to Isla. "Bogi will guard the front door. Stay here inside until we get back, understand?"

"I'm not leaving," she replied. "We'll be in our room."

Ashley quickly retrieved her gun from the hidden cabinet inside the kitchen hutch, then glanced at Cade. "I'll stay with them and Ozzy can stand guard with the officer watching their room."

Cade kissed her on the cheek. "We'll see about this. Could be tourists out on a ride. If not, we'll try to hold them off."

"Be careful," she replied, hugging him close.

Cade held her tight, then pulled away and glanced down at her stomach before he looked back at her. "You, too."

Isla's heart beat a swift warning. She could feel her pulse pushing through every vein in her body. She held Enzo as he cooed at a stuffed teddy bear, her prayers caught in a web of fear.

Ashley and the officer by their door kept checking on Bogi for signals of stress or to alert them. Isla hoped he wouldn't let anyone come through this house.

Granny sat still, her eyes closed as her

lips moved in an ongoing prayer. Ashley came into the bedroom and sat by the window, her phone on the table, her gun in her hand.

"Bear," Enzo said, giggling as he held the little blue animal up to Isla. "Mama, bear."

"That is a bear," she said, kissing his dark curls. His big brown eyes held such trust she almost lost her breath. "Enzo's bear."

"Mine," Enzo said, snuggling close to her with a breakfast cracker in one hand. Thankful she had some snacks for him in a bag on the dresser, she'd feed him a real meal later. She couldn't think beyond that one thought—they'd have a later.

"Mine," she replied, hoping Enzo would truly be hers soon.

"No movement so far," Ashley said after lifting back a curtain to check the area around the barn. "But we have people stationed in the trees, watching."

They sat quietly, waiting for what seemed like hours, but really had only been a few minutes. When Isla thought she'd scream from the pressure, they heard gunfire echoing over the hills and woods. Several shots in rapid succession.

Then a crash sounded outside the house. Ozzy started barking and Bogi's hard growl echoed across to the hallway.

"Stay down." Ashley crouched by one of the windows facing north from where the shots had come. The officer in the hallway opened the bedroom door. "I'll lock this door and check the perimeters."

Ashley nodded and silenced Ozzy. Isla heard noises, footsteps and what sounded like a scuffle near one of the bedroom windows. Then there was another crash as a gunshot pinged and glass from the shattered window went all over the room.

Granny kept praying and slid into the corner. Isla dropped behind a chair and held so tight to Enzo, he pushed away and squirmed out of her arms and wobbled toward the glass-covered floor.

"Enzo," she whispered, trying to grab him as cold air filled the room. She stayed down and belly crawled on the floor and rolled a ball toward him. "Bring it to Mommy," she said in a wobbly plea. "Pretty please."

He picked up the ball and threw it. The shattered window jiggled. Isla glanced at Ashley. Her friend put a finger to her lips and moved toward the window. Ozzy was ready to attack on her order. Bogi barked loudly now and snarled.

Isla managed to grab Enzo, her heartbeat sounding through her ears, while the intruder kept pushing at what was left of the window. Then they heard a distinctive sound. The sound of another round being put into the gun's chamber.

Ashley braced herself, her gun aimed at the broken window. Ozzy stood still, his focus on the intruder.

The tension in the room stretched like a cable wire about to pop. Enzo gazed at Isla. Then he burst into loud sobs.

Isla gritted her teeth and hugged him tight, knowing they could all be shot. Then came a shout from outside. "Riders on horseback. Let's get out of here."

The footsteps departed toward the back of the house, followed by more shots ringing across the countryside like fireworks.

Ashley crawled to the window and peeked

out a sliver in the curtains. "I see our men. We're safe."

"For now," Isla said in a whisper, her arms wrapped around her son. But not for long, she knew.

Michael rushed inside the house and gave Bogi the clear sign, then rushed down the hallway, the intense dog behind him. "Isla?"

"We're here," she called as he whirled by the officer who'd returned inside. "We're all here."

He rushed to her and pulled Enzo into his arms. "Are you all right?"

"We're okay," she said, nodding, her dark eyes filled with relief. "You?"

He held the child close, relief washing over him. "We're good. We chased two off before they made it to the house. Checked the woods and put out alerts, then shot at the two trying to get into the house. Last we saw, an official SUV was chasing them up the highway."

"But they got away?" Ashley asked as Cade held her tight.

"For now," Michael replied. "They now know the ranch is being heavily guarded."

"Did they see you?" Isla asked.

"No. We were hidden behind some trees, waiting for them to approach, an Elk Valley Police SUV blocking their way."

"That and a few rifle shots did the trick," Cade said. "We held them off, but we can't be sure they'll stay away. They were trespassing but that won't matter much with this kind."

"Nothing matters to these kind," Granny said from her corner. "Evil to go after someone who is innocent."

She glanced from Isla to Michael, the meaning behind her statement clear to all of them.

Michael lifted his chin and returned her glance. "You're right. This has to end. And I'm the only one who can make it stop."

ELEVEN

"What does that mean?" Isla asked a few minutes later after they'd been cleared to come back to the den. "Don't do anything to put yourself in danger."

"I'm putting you and all these people in danger," he said, already pulling away. "I thought I could get you away safely. But now, this thing keeps escalating. They will be relentless because they've failed. It's a matter of power and pride now."

And he still hadn't heard a word from Dillon Sellers. "I'm afraid they've already taken out Dillon. If they have, then they probably have all the information they need on me, too."

"Call someone else," she said. "You can't go all noble on me now, Michael."

"I'm not the noble kind," he replied. "I

can't call anyone else. Top secret and too risky. I think Dillon sent Bogi to me because someone on that base is connected to Saconni. Like I said before, we need that one more piece of the puzzle to figure this out."

"Then you stay put until I can dig some more," she said, the look in her eyes daring him to make a move. "You walk now and you risk the lives of everyone here protecting us. Neither of us could live with that." Glancing around to where Granny stood helping Ashley make sandwiches, she said, "But this has gone from protecting a K-9 to finding out what these people really want. And I can help with that. It's my job."

Michael paced, his head down, his mind whirling. "Do one more search to see if any of your connections can come up with something. If we don't get anything by tomorrow night, I'm moving you and your family again."

Isla nodded and headed straight to the corner desk. "I'll be over here until Enzo wakes up from his afternoon nap."

He nodded, then pulled out one of the

three burner phones he had. Ashley had called in a report to Chase and he would update the police chief. Michael tried one more time to reach Dillon, using an old number he'd memorized years ago. Still no answer, but at least the number seemed to work. It wasn't like Dillon to ghost him, but then again they hadn't had an opportunity to talk much when Michael had gone to a deserted airstrip to pick up Bogi. Dillon and the pilot he'd hired had been waiting and they'd gotten Bogi on the plane pretty quickly with nothing more than a "thanks and I owe you one" from Dillon.

He went over to Isla. "Anything?"

She turned to him and nodded, then looked over at the others. "We need to talk."

He sat down beside her. "What?"

"I got a hit from a source in Europe. Another shell company with a branch right here in Wyoming. River Purses. Ever heard of it?"

Michael's mind buzzed like a bumblebee. "Yes, I have heard of it." His stomach roiled as the puzzle seemed ready to fall into place. "I can't remember where."

Isla's eyes lit up but held a track of fear. "The name Saconni is a variation on *saccone*, which mean *maker of purses.* River Purses manufacture Italian leather goods— expensive handbags, like maybe thousands of dollars for each purse."

"Okay, so what's that got to do with us and this case?"

"A lot. The Saconni cartel owns River Purses. It's one of their deeply buried shell companies, but there is a River Purses store in Laramie. I looked it up. They are all over social media, selling all kinds of leather goods, even coats and jackets."

"Okay, tell me more," he said, that sick feeling settling in his gut.

"My source says that's a cover and a way to lure people into selling drugs. He says this cartel has a wide reach from America to Europe and South America, which means the store here must cater to rich clients and vulnerable people who want to be like those rich clients."

He studied her face, thinking she was so beautiful, and so smart. "And that could mean they definitely have a stash house here and plenty of loyal underlings who'd do anything to win favor."

"Yes," she said. "Should we visit that store?"

"No. Too dangerous." He held a hand to his head, memories misting just out of his reach. "I wish I could remember where I heard about these purses. It must have been someone I know because I don't go purse shopping a lot."

Isla touched her hand to his. "Maybe it will come to you. The good news is we can put surveillance on that particular store, see who's coming and going."

"Good idea."

"I've also been searching Bogi's background since you and he left the military," she said. "He wasn't always back at Lackland. For a while after he retired as a war dog, Dillon had him, and interesting thing—according to his vet records, that's when Bogi became even more aggressive." She took a breath and looked down to where Bogi sat, guarding. "This dog hasn't been aggressive, not once since I've been around him. I'd trust him with

Enzo. I'd trust him to alert because I believe he knows the truth, too."

Michael's brain dinged and pinged with reality. "You think Dillon has something to do with all of this, right? You've been leaning toward that angle since I told you about him."

"I'm following the leads and yes, this one stands out to me. He is your only source of information and yet, you can't get in touch with him. Think about that, Michael."

Michael had to agree with her, whether he liked it or not. "If Bogi has heard or seen something that brings out his aggressive nature, he can't really show or tell us that until we have this figured out."

"Yes, because alerting is his only way of telling us the truth," she replied.

Michael stared at the K-9, then looked back at Isla, his mind reeling. "But who? And where and when will he be able to do that?"

"Only Dillon can help us there," she said. "And he's missing in action."

Michael told Chase he wasn't leaving the ranch again. He and Isla pulled the information they'd found and Isla saved it on a tiny flash drive and hid it in the desk drawer, taped inside a box of envelopes. Michael still couldn't remember where he'd heard about River Purses but figured it had to be from someone he knew. But mostly, his mind couldn't accept that his friend and former teammate might have betrayed him. Yet the puzzle pieces were beginning to fit.

"They're tracking us somehow," he reminded Isla at the dinner table that night. Annette and Enzo had gone to bed, while Isla and he sat with Cade and Ashley. He glanced at Bogi. "I wish he could tell us what he knows."

As if on cue, Bogi grunted and scratched at his collar.

Isla looked at the dog and then back to him. Ashley gave Bogi a curious stare. "He scratches at that collar a lot, you know."

Isla let out a gasp. "What if they put a tracker on Bogi?"

Ashley nodded. "I was thinking the same thing."

Michael called the dog to his side. "I haven't given him much attention since this happened, but I have noticed him always pulling and scratching at his collar. That makes perfect sense."

Michael lifted the heavy brown leather collar and undid it, then ran his hand over the worn back side. Silently, he pointed to a small flat button embedded between the leather and the metal label on the front. He didn't put the collar back on. "This is how they've been able to get to us."

Later that night, Cade and Michael slipped out with Bogi wearing the tracker. At a neighbor's remote ranch, and with his permission, they'd taken it off Bogi and placed it on a long bridle around a mean bull's massive neck. Ashley had followed to make it look like everyone in the house would be moving on and they'd left her SUV at the other ranch.

"That will keep them guessing for days," Michael told her after they'd returned. "We got a call from the hired hands guarding the woods. They heard motors cranking and off-road vehicles leaving the premises, so the patrols up on the road will coordinate with Cade's friend and hopefully capture a few of our lurkers."

Now, two nights later, Isla sat with Michael on the sofa, the house quiet and the fire mostly embers, but she couldn't get over the jitters. Or the way Michael made her feel when they were alone like this.

"So nothing's happened since you removed the tracker. Could this finally be over?"

"Not yet. We did capture two of them trying to sneak onto the other property, but we need to locate their headquarters. We've got them busy and confused but the two in jail aren't talking."

While the quiet times had been nice and she'd felt safe again, Isla wanted to go home. "We still need to be careful. That's why we have a guard, right?"

"Yes," Michael said. "I've lost my edge. I didn't consider them putting a bug on Bogi. I don't think I've thanked you at all for figuring that out." He looked over at her, their gazes clashing. "I don't think I've thanked you for any of this. So thank you, Isla."

"It's about time," she replied with a muster of snark, her heart hammering. She liked being close to him but it was also torment. "Maybe now at least we can finish this up."

"We have some other things to finish, too," he said, leaning close. "Like this." He kissed her, his warm lips touching hers with such a gentle sweep, she couldn't help but sigh and kiss him back. They both pulled away, awe crackling between them like kindling starting a fire.

"A nice surprise—that's what you are," he whispered as he reached for her again. "I like sitting by the fire with you."

Bogi suddenly jumped up and stood, his whole body trembling.

"Maybe he's jealous," Michael teased.

The big dog growled and stared down the hallway. They heard a pop and Michael grabbed her. "Silencer," he whispered.

Ozzy started barking.

Isla twisted away, panic in her eyes. "Granny?" She rushed to the bedroom and opened the door, then screamed.

Michael and Bogi ran in, Ashley, Michael and Ozzy right behind them. Isla was kneeling on the floor, sobbing. "They're gone," she shouted, looking up at him. "Gone."

Michael scanned the empty room and saw a blue teddy bear lying by the crib, his heart bursting with a pain like none he'd ever felt before. Enzo loved that teddy bear.

"Isla," he said, bending and reaching out to her. "Isla, I'm so sorry."

"Get away from me," she screamed as the others gathered in the room. "Where is the guard, where is my protection? You promised me, Michael. You promised me."

Still sobbing, she pushed past all of them and ran out into the night. "Enzo, Enzo. Where are you?"

Michael watched, her pain cutting him like a knife. Then he turned and saw a figure lying on the ground by two Adirondack chairs. He hurried and turned over the still body. The patrol officer who'd been guarding the door lay dead, a bullet wound in his temple, his own gun still clutched in his hand.

And suddenly, Michael remembered where he'd seen a River Purse. Dillon Sellers's latest girlfriend had been holding one when he'd last visited Dillon about a year ago, before any of this had happened. The purse had been rich brown leather, but with a bright red emblem that had reminded him of a clear-shot wound. Just like the one on this officer's forehead.

He looked at Isla as Ashley tried to comfort her, then he turned to where Bogi stood growling and shaking with rage. Michael commanded the K-9 to come, then stalked out to his Jeep and left. He planned to find Dillon Sellers and make him pay, and he had no problem dying in order to seek justice. What did he have to live for if Isla had lost her family because of him?

Isla sat on the bed, the blue teddy bear clutched to her chest. She couldn't sleep, couldn't eat, didn't want to talk to anyone at all. Ashley kept checking on her, and finally came in and sat beside her without saying a word. They both started crying.

"I don't think I can live," Isla whispered. "I've survived a lot of things, but I don't think I can survive this."

Ashley only nodded. Then she whispered back, "We have search parties everywhere, looking. The flash drive with the information on Saconni is with Chase now—good thing you told me where you'd hidden it. That information could lead us right to them. We've got people watching their store."

Isla tried to speak, but her sobs increased. "Where is Michael?" Not that she wanted to see him again, but he'd left without a word. Did she want that? To *never* see him again?

She only wanted her Granny Annie and Enzo safe. After that, she didn't care. At all. She'd get out of this bed and find them her way.

Ashley didn't answer her question.

"Where is he?" Isla repeated, her voice rising this time.

Ashley gave her a level stare. "He's doing what he needs to do. He's heard from the cartel, so he's meeting them tonight to hand over Bogi in exchange for your grandmother and Enzo."

"What?" Isla got up and started putting on her clothes. "Take me there now, Ashley.

I have to get to them." When Ashley didn't readily agree, she said, "I know who's behind this. It's not the cartel, but Dillon Sellers. He's been running the whole show, but I can't prove that."

Ashley stood, her phone out. "Chase needs to hear this."

"No, Chase needs to take me there. I mean it. If he doesn't, I'll find out where they are and go alone."

TWELVE

Two hours later, Michael sat in his Jeep with Bogi, tapping his fingers on the worn leather steering wheel. He had to do this. Had to give over Bogi to save Annette and Enzo. He hadn't slept since last night after he'd gotten the call he'd been waiting for.

"Mr. Tanner," the smooth accented voice had said. "I see you've wised up now that we have collateral damage to discuss."

"I'm wise to you," Michael told the man. "The dog for the woman and child. See how easy that was."

"Smart decision." The man had named the place and the time.

After that, Michael had geared up back at his place only to find two of Elk Valley's best along with Chase, waiting for him.

"You're not doing this alone," Chase said, shaking his head.

"I have to. They've made that clear without even reminding me. Do you want Annette and that little boy to die?"

"No, what I want is for you to be sensible so nobody will get killed."

They had a SWAT team lined up, and they'd called in some favors. Several K-9 officers from other units would slip through the woods and be ready to help the SWAT team.

After Chase threatened to lock him up, Michael finally agreed. He couldn't exactly take down more than a half-dozen people and he had no idea how many would be waiting for him.

For once, he wasn't going rogue. He had to do this by the book. He checked his watch and got out of the Jeep, Bogi jumping out behind him. He walked up to a dark building that looked like a giant garage and waited about ten yards from the front door.

When a lone man came out that door, Michael wasn't surprised at all. But he sure wished he'd listened to Isla about this.

Dillon Sellers stood dressed in a black leather jacket and black jeans. "MT, you finally decided to do the right thing."

"Nice jacket," Michael replied, his gut burning with a heated rage, his plan to follow the rules going up in smoke. "I'm guessing that's the kind of jacket I'd find in a River Purse store?"

"They do sell all kinds of goods, yes."

Bogi growled and lifted up with a snarl, but Michael held him by the new protective working collar and vest he'd put on him earlier. "I see Bogi and you aren't on good terms anymore."

"Nope. Bogi knows too much about the cartel and, well, about me."

"Because you're the one, aren't you?" Michael asked. "The one who made sure I'd get the wrong intel on that mission and cause innocents to die. Just like you've done with this whole mess we have now."

"No, I made sure you had the best intel to get that stupid mission over with and done. You always were a softy."

"So if you kill Bogi and me, no one can ever prove you set me up to take the blame for all those deaths."

"You got it, buddy." Dillon glanced back. "That and I get a sweet deal. Two million in cash—double the original asking price."

"Why not turn him over yourself? You'd still get the reward."

"Because it would be too obvious—he's only aggressive around me. I sent him on that last mission, thinking he'd get shot, but no, he had to become a national hero. I decided to get you two back together, kill two birds with one stone and end this thing that's been hanging over me for years."

"Why not take us both out when we met at the plane?" Michael asked.

"Too many eyes, even if that place did seem deserted," Dillon replied. "It would have been too obvious."

The puzzle pieces had finally fallen into place.

Michael stared at the man who'd once been his best friend. "So after all this time, you decided it was time to end the very things that have also haunted me for years.

Let me guess—Bogi was about to give you away because he always alerted around you."

"Sorry, but I can't have you and that dog undermining my position now, can I?"

"No, but positions come and go," Michael said. "Before I hand over Bogi, I need proof of life."

Dillon gave a signal to someone at the open door of the big building. Michael held his breath when he saw Annette coming out with Enzo in her arms, her expression cold and blank.

He lifted his chin to Dillon. "This is it, Bogi. Goodbye, boy." Then he leaned down and let go. "Attack."

Dillon shouted as Bogi lunged toward him. Then the woods went wild with barking dogs and camouflaged officers. Gunfire hissed and sizzled through the cold black night. Michael didn't call Bogi off. The sound of Dillon's screams merged with the team rushing into the building. Michael stood and watched the K-9 he'd trusted with his life finally giving him the answers he'd always needed.

Chase came rushing up. "Michael, call off your dog."

Michael glared at his friend and then shouted, "Let go."

Bogi dropped Dillon like a sack of potatoes and stood still, guarding, while Dillon wailed and tried to get away. Chase handed Michael the cuffs.

"This is for all the people who died," he said on a hiss as he grabbed and handcuffed the man who was once his best friend. "And for Bogi, a better officer than you could ever be."

Back in the SUV where Chase had left her and Ashley, Isla heard all the noise and jumped out of the vehicle. She couldn't stay put, knowing her little boy and the grandmother she loved so much were in danger.

And Michael. She had to see Michael.

Ashley called after her, but she kept running toward the noise of barking K-9s. A sound like music to her ears.

By the time she got there, it was over.

She saw Granny and Enzo standing off to the side with Chase. "Granny! Enzo!"

Chase whirled and glared but didn't say anything. He watched as she hugged her sweet little boy and her amazing grandmother, tears of relief falling down her cheeks. Glancing around, her head held against Enzo's, she spotted Michael.

He nodded then turned and walked away, Bogi by his side.

Two days later, Isla hurried out the door with Enzo and Granny, praying she'd still be able to officially adopt the toddler. They were headed to the courthouse to make her longtime dream come true. If it *would*. Fatigue tugged at her brain. She hadn't slept well, but then she never did. And she hadn't heard a word from Michael Tanner.

Dillon Sellers was in jail, and most of the cartel members had scattered after Rico Saconni had tried to escape the stash house where they'd held her family. He been caught hiding in a shed, K-9s barking all around him. He'd go to prison along with Dillon.

She wanted to talk to Michael.

Not that she expected to see him again.

She'd told him to leave her alone and blamed him for her grandmother and son being taken, but now she regretted being so cruel to him. In the end, he hadn't gone rogue. He'd gone against his grain to save her family—and Bogi, too.

Only a good man would do something so heroic and noble. Only a good man would kiss her with such tenderness, he'd melted the walls around her heart.

But only Michael would do that and walk away because he didn't think he was worthy of a family. She'd believed that about herself once, but she knew they were both worthy.

She'd gotten Enzo strapped into his car seat when a blue pickup truck pulled up to the curb.

Michael.

He got out and walked up to her. "Hi."

"Hi," she said, glancing to where Granny sat in the back of her small SUV with Enzo. "What are you doing here?"

"I came to go with you to court. Annette called me."

Isla glanced back at her grandmother.

Annette shrugged and nodded. Not sure how to react, Isla studied his face.

"I would have been there anyway," he clarified. "But I want to drive you there. If you'll let me."

She tossed him the keys and went around to the passenger's seat. "Let's go."

When they got to the courthouse, Isla's nerves had reached a high pitch, but with Granny on one side and Michael on the other, she held her child close and held her head high.

Then when they got inside and she saw the whole K-9 team and most of the police force, including Nora Quan, there waiting, tears fell down her cheeks.

The judge took note and listened as Chase, Michael and Nora all explained what had happened and how Isla had fought so hard for those she loved. The judge had tears in her eyes by the time everyone had given their testimonies, and the adoption went through without a hitch.

She was Enzo's mother now.

After they filed out, sniffing and crying

and hugging, Granny invited everyone for an early Christmas dinner. "I've been cooking for days, so you can't say no."

They all showed up at her house at about the same time snow started falling in beautiful big flakes. After putting Enzo down for his nap, Isla stood inside the short hallway and marveled at all the wonderful friends in her life.

Michael had been quiet, but he and his shadow, K-9 Bogi, approached her. "Can we talk?" he asked, motioning toward the backyard.

She put on her coat and followed them out, then turned to face him, her heart so scattered and shattered, she wasn't sure if it could ever have a normal beat again.

"You have your family now," he began, his words jittery and his expression bordering on panic. "But I was wondering. I mean Bogi and I were wondering…"

"Yes?"

"You're not going to make this easy, are you?"

"Easy?" She laughed. "Nothing has been

easy with you, Michael." Then she tugged him close. "Except that kiss."

He grinned, relief washing through his eyes. Eyes that held honesty now, and hope. "I wondered if you might find it in your heart to forgive me and let me and Bogi hang around?"

"That depends," she replied. "Will you disappear in the night to do all your spy things? Or can I depend on you to hang around for a long time?"

He smiled and held her there. "I'm a veterinarian full-time now. No more nefarious missions. I'm here to stay."

Bogi barked in agreement and rolled in the snow.

Isla kissed Michael and then touched a hand to the map that was his face. "I'd like that, Michael. I'd like that a lot."

"I'd like that, too," he said, no more secrets shadowing his eyes. "And I think I love you. A lot."

Isla opened her heart. "I think I love you back. A lot."

They kissed, then the back door burst

open and the team got involved in a snow-ball fight, dogs included.

Granny brought Enzo out all bundled up and handed him to Isla, then turned to Michael. "Remember what I told you."

"Always," he replied, saluting Granny.

"What did she say?" Isla asked.

"She said it in Spanish, but I'm pretty sure she explained how she'd hurt me in bad ways if I break your heart."

"You won't do that," Isla told him. "I trust you, Michael."

And she knew it was true. Her spy had come in from the cold and she had a family to love, a family full of faithful guardians. The best Christmas present ever.

* * * * *

*If you enjoyed this story, don't miss
the rest of the action-packed
Mountain Country K-9 Unit series!*

Baby Protection Mission
by Laura Scott, April 2024

Her Duty Bound Defender
by Sharee Stover, May 2024

Chasing Justice
by Valerie Hansen, June 2024

Crime Scene Secrets
by Maggie K. Black, July 2024

Montana Abduction Rescue
by Jodie Bailey, August 2024

Trail of Threats
by Jessica R. Patch, September 2024

Tracing a Killer
by Sharon Dunn, October 2024

Search and Detect
by Terri Reed, November 2024

Christmas K-9 Guardians
by Lenora Worth and Katy Lee,
December 2024

Available only from
Love Inspired Suspense.
Discover more at LoveInspired.com

Dear Reader,

I loved writing this story of a hero war dog and a tormented human veteran who turned to animals for comfort when the human world let him down. Earlier this year, we got a tiny puppy and I named him Bogi—because he's part Yorkie, Maltese and Shih Tzu. So that made me think of *The Maltese Falcon*, one of my favorite books, and Humphrey Bogart, who starred in the movie. Little Bogi has a ferocious bark, but his bites are not harmful. He follows us around and is always ready to play a game of fetch, but hasn't learned to return whatever needs fetching.

His unconditional love makes us smile and calms us when we're having a bad day. I wanted that same comfort for my characters, Michael and Isla. If you've read this whole series, you've seen Isla in action, doing her job and trying to adopt a child. She never gave up and when Michael needed her help, she did her best and risked everything to find the people after Bogi and him.

I know God wants to offer us that kind of comfort—the unconditional love, the peace beyond understanding and the hope that brings about a calm that guards and protects our hearts.

Until next time, may the angels watch over you. Always.
Lenora

LETHAL HOLIDAY HIDEOUT

Katy Lee

To Isabella, my groupie leader
and motivational mate of all the things.
I'm so thankful God brought you into my life.

Acknowledgments

I want to thank my new editor, Katie Gowrie,
for her enthusiasm about my work. I'm excited to create
more wonderful books with her in the future. Her
dedication and commitment to bring wonderful stories
to our readers only make our books shine even more.

I also want to thank K-9 trainers for their time and
investment into these powerful and intelligent dogs,
particularly the K-9 unit at Hill Air Force Base
for their willingness to demonstrate and
share their skills with me.

Commit thy works unto the Lord,
and thy thoughts shall be established.
The Lord hath made all things for himself.
—*Proverbs* 16:3–4

ONE

"Mocha, down!" Special Agent Cara Haines, Washington, DC, and K-9 Task Force boss, ordered the unruly chocolate Labrador to quit jumping and barking in her crate. At this rate, the dog would never qualify for the Mountain Country K-9 Unit that Cara oversaw. She righted her glasses that had slipped when wrestling the dog inside the vehicle and prepared to lower the SUV's rear door. She had taken Mocha to the outdoor training facility in Alexandria for some exercise and fresh air, not ready to give up on the recruit. Being December, the K-9s did most of their training on the inside course, but Cara thought a change of scenery would do Mocha good. Cara wasn't sure if the dog was going to pass the assessment to become a full-fledged K-9 officer.

The dog's rambunctiousness told Cara she might be sadly right.

However, Mocha wasn't the only one who needed some fresh air that day. Cara needed a little breather from her stuffy city office as well. She spent most of her days on conference calls and doing paperwork up to the top of her six-foot frame, rarely having time with the dogs anymore. Ten years ago, she gave up being a trainer out west and took on the role of the big boss in the FBI DC offices, overseeing task forces around the country instead. Some days, she just wanted to be with the dogs—she *needed* to be with them, even the unruly K-9s. Today was one of those days.

Last week, Cara received a notification that her ex-brother-in-law would be released from prison this week. The state of California reduced his twenty-year sentence to ten. Cara angrily thought of all she had given up because of that man. Moving her home across the country from Wyoming to DC was only one of them.

Mocha continued to whimper but still strained to be released from the confines of the back of the FBI SUV. Her black eyes alerted on something in the vicinity.

Perhaps there was more to Mocha's rambunctiousness than Cara realized.

"What do you see, girl?" Cara's own senses spiked and the hair on the back of her neck stood to attention. She flipped the safety strap on the holster beneath her black suit coat and had her weapon in her palm before she turned and raised it.

Every corner of the outdoor facility remained empty.

Cara's gaze darted to each structure and obstacle of the fenced-in course. Tires, boxes, jump poles became places to hide behind. Cara targeted her focus on the shadows the structures caused. As far as she could tell, there was no sign of anyone else around. The outdoor course wasn't as protected as the official training center, and she thought she might need to change that in the future. Anyone could easily get in here.

But it didn't appear anyone had. As best as she could see, she remained alone.

Cara lowered her gun and reholstered it.

She left the flap undone just in case she needed a quick draw again. Turning back to the dog, she reached to close the rear hatch.

"False alerting is not a good sign for you, Mocha." She issued a warning to the dog and pushed the button to close the door. Cara came around to the driver's door, but before she opened it, a firm hand went around her mouth. Her back hit against a hard chest. She went for her gun but found the holster empty. She heard the gun hit the ground, leaving her weaponless.

Mocha jumped around in her crate, barking profusely inside the SUV, now useless to Cara. Whoever this man was, he recognized the need to wait to make his move until she'd secured the dog.

A pocketknife appeared in front of her face in the man's other hand. One flick and the four-inch blade opened inches from her nose.

At fifty-two years of age, thirty of which were in law enforcement, she didn't think she'd ever been in this situation. Decades of technical practice and self-defense classes rushed to the forefront of her mind, but none of them prepared her for the real thing. Cara knew she had seconds to live if she didn't kick her mind into gear.

Kick was the operative word, she thought.

"We're going to do this slow and easy," the man said in a low voice. "One wrong move and I will slit your throat. Simple as that."

Cara tried to breathe deeply through her nose, but his thumb covered one of her nostrils, making it difficult to fill her lungs. Remaining calm was her only choice. She nodded her compliance once.

"Good. You're a smart woman. Smarter than your sister."

So this was about her sister. The sister Cara hadn't seen in ten years. If Cara didn't know better, she'd think this man was her ex-brother-in-law. But he was still behind bars, so how could it be him?

"You're going to take me to her."

Cara shook her head as much as she could. His request was impossible. She tried to speak through his hand pressed against her lips. At the shake of her head, he brought the knife closer.

"You don't get to choose." The knife came away from her face, and the next thing she heard was the clinking sound of her handcuffs removed from her belt. She had no more time to wait to make her move. If this man apprehended her and stuffed her in her car, there was no telling where he would take her next.

Closing her eyes, she pulled on the memories of breaking out of a person's hold. With the knife gone, she used her foot to find his instep. With as much breath as she could take in, Cara grunted and stepped down on his inner ankle, twisting around at the same moment to grab his arm and flip him. In less than five seconds, she threw him to the ground, ripped the handcuffs from his hand and slapped one cuff on his wrist.

The man struggled and squirmed. Suddenly, with his free hand, he reached for her gun on the ground. Cara lunged forward to beat him to it, but just as she grabbed the handle of the gun, he seized the barrel.

She let go of the cuffs to fight him for

the gun, spotting another officer entering the facility.

"Stand down!" The young woman rookie officer raced in with her own gun drawn.

The perpetrator let go of Cara's gun for his knife. Before Cara knew what he planned, he threw the blade in her direction just as the rookie's gun discharged.

Cara ducked as fast as she could, but the knife sliced through the shoulder of her suit coat, throwing her body back against the car.

As the echo of the blast died down, and Cara regrouped over what had just happened, the man lay dead in front of her.

"Are you okay? Don't move!" The woman crouched in front of Cara, unsure of what to do with the knife protruding from Cara's shoulder.

"Kick the gun away," Cara instructed her. "Just in case." Although judging by the way his eyes were wide with no life in them, she knew the girl's shot had been accurate.

The rookie called for an ambulance while Cara examined the protruding knife, expecting only minor tissue damage. Mocha jumped around in her cage. Cara knew she might hurt herself if she wasn't informed that the perpetrator had been silenced.

"Open the back door and try to calm her down," Cara said through clenched teeth. Pain set in with a slow burn. She glanced at the rookie's name on her badge. "And thank you, Officer Vasquez. Good work today. I'd say I probably owe you my life."

"Not necessarily, ma'am. I'm sure you'd have taken him down at any moment." The young woman smiled, allowing Cara to keep her pride intact. "Do you know what he wanted?"

"Yeah. He wanted my sister, and he wanted me to lead her to her."

"Well, I'm glad your sister's still safe. And you too. Wait until you tell her you saved her life today."

Cara frowned, knowing that conversation would never happen. "I saved her life ten years ago by getting her into the witness protection program."

Vasquez gasped at what that statement meant. A sad expression settled on her face. "That must've been a hard decision to make."

"It was the only decision to make. Her husband was Luis Morel."

The woman's eyes widened. "The head of the Mexican mob? How did your sister get mixed up with him? That organization is more dangerous than any cartel. They run every gang in California's prisons."

"And most likely the guards too, if Morel's made parole. My sister met him on vacation down in Mexico. She didn't know who he was until after she was married and living with him in California four weeks later. With over fifty thousand foot soldiers and assassins at his disposal all over the continent, I had no choice but to let her go into Witness Protection. He would have killed her, and not before torturing her."

The woman looked at the dead guy. Her face blanched. "You think Morel sent this man?"

The ambulance's siren rang off in the distance. She'd take the ride to get stitched up, but that would be it. "I don't *think* Morel sent this man. I *know* he did."

"Do you think your sister's still safe?"

Cara reached for her cell phone inside her coat. With her good hand, she thumb-dialed the only person who would know the answer to that question.

The phone rang three times before US Marshal Sullivan Briggs answered the call. "I'm surprised to see your number on my caller ID, Cara." His deep voice rumbled through her speaker. It still had a way of soothing her nerves, but she wouldn't tell him that. "I'm surprised you even remembered my number. How long has it been since you called?"

His cynicism was anything *but* soothing.

Cara ignored his question and cut right to the chase. "I was just attacked by one of Morel's men. Luis will be out of prison this week, and he's already looking for my sister. You need to find out if she's safe right now and make sure she has a detail on her."

"Attacked? Are you okay?" Sully sounded stunned through the line.

She glanced at the knife protruding out of her left shoulder. "I'll need stitches, but that's nothing to what Jeanette will need if

Morel gets ahold of her. Call her handler right now."

"I'm making the call as we speak. But are *you* safe? I want the truth, Cara."

"He's dead." She left out the part about nearly being taken out by him. Cara could kick herself. She'd let her guard down when she should have been expecting something from Morel.

"There'll be more coming, Cara. You know it."

"Yeah, but I'll be ready next time. What have you heard? Did you reach her handler?"

"Hold on. I'm trying his other number."

The paramedics pulled in and before Cara knew it, she was being lowered onto the stretcher, carefully on her good side. Her adrenaline still surged as she waited for the answer.

"Answer me, Sully. That's an order!" She bit back the pain radiating through her body. A weakness overcame her, causing dizziness. Shock, maybe, she thought. Minor wound or not, she was losing blood.

"An order?" Sully chuckled, which only

grated on her nerves more. "He'll call me back soon, I'm sure. Don't worry. Your sister has been safe for ten years. She's happy doing what she loves most. I made sure I assigned her a good life she could love. You just need to make sure you're safe."

"I'm coming out there." Cara felt her weakening body lifting into the ambulance. She grunted with the landing. "As soon as I get this knife out of me," she mumbled.

The line went quiet. Then Sully said, "Neither of those statements makes me feel good. First, you stay right where you are in DC. You can't know where your sister is, so there is no reason to come out to Wyoming."

The paramedics in front of her blurred and when she spoke, her tongue got in the way. "I have to…" The rest of her sentence made no sense, even to her ears.

"Put the paramedic on the phone, Cara. Now!" Sully demanded.

Cara heard him speaking somewhere in the darkness of unconsciousness, but she couldn't form any more words.

"Cara! Don't leave me!" he shouted.

But somewhere in her mind, she knew those words weren't said by him today.

Those were the words Sully said to her ten years ago when she did just that.

TWO

Sully hung up one phone, only to make another call to Logan Doyle. At this rate, he'd have an entire head of gray hair by tomorrow morning. Jeanette Morel, now known as Jennie Monet, had lived out in Jackson, Wyoming for the last ten years, without a hint of a problem. Sully had put his best man in the role as Jennie's handler, but now Logan had yet to answer any of his calls. Sully reasoned that the handler would have a good explanation for ignoring his calls.

Except Cara had just had surgery after being stabbed by one of Morel's men. Not to mention the fact that if her attacker knew where her sister was living, he wouldn't have needed Cara to begin with. As far as Sully was concerned, Jennie was still in expert hands.

And so was Cara.

The doctor had assured Sully that Cara was stable now. Her surgery had been smooth, and she was resting.

Sully chuckled at the term the doctor used. *Stable* was not a word Sully would link with Cara Haines. The word *stable* reminded him of something uneventful, predictable, maybe even boring.

No, Cara had never been boring and never would be. But that didn't mean her life had always been secure. Sully knew all the strife that Cara had had to grow up with, forcing her into a role as guardian for her little sister. An absent mother and a drunken father had led Cara through a life of hard knocks and an unhealthy need for control over every aspect of her being. But never one to let her past define her future, Cara became the best cop Sully had ever met. She was by the book, never wavering from doing what was right. Even saying goodbye to her sister forever to keep her safe.

That ultimate act from the big sister put

Sully in awe of Cara. He just never thought she would leave him because of it.

Sully thought back to when he had first partnered with Cara, long before she oversaw the Mountain Country K-9 Unit, which he still partnered with. Ten years ago, Cara had been a supervisor with the Wyoming FBI, quickly rising high in the ranks because of her diligence and expertise in the department. When DC offered her the position as the big boss at FBI headquarters, she'd shrugged it off and kissed him, assuring him she wasn't going anywhere. Then Luis Morel entered their lives and destroyed everything.

But then, Morel didn't break them up. Cara did that all on her own.

As a US Marshal supervisor, Sully would always know Jennie's location and identity in witness protection, and he could never tell Cara. Just as Cara was by the book, so was he. She'd said there couldn't be two big bosses in the relationship. So DC became her next rank, and he was relegated to part of her past.

Sully's cell phone rang on his desk. He

glanced quickly, but it wasn't Logan. Instead, the number alerted Sully to Chase Rawlston, the MCK9 task force leader. Sully accepted the call.

"I'm assuming you heard about Cara," he said before Chase wasted his breath on relaying the message. The sound of Christmas music wafted through the phone line. "Sounds like the office is getting ready for the holidays." A glance around his own drab office at the Cheyenne US Marshals building made him wonder if he should hang something to recognize the upcoming day next week. After all, it was his Savior's birthday. Maybe a few brightly colored lights around the door would liven the place up.

"How are you holding up?" Chase asked.

"Me?" Surprised, Sully cleared his throat. But what would be the sense of denying the stress he'd experienced that day? How he had stayed on the phone with the paramedics for the longest twenty-five minutes of his life, and how he had barked at the doctor to hurry and get Cara into surgery.

"She's going to live. That's all that matters," Sully said.

"I heard. She just called me."

"Did she really?" Despite having no reason for the surprise, Sully huffed in disbelief. "The woman just got out of surgery. What's she thinking?"

"You know Cara, nothing keeps her down. She'll most likely work right through Christmas and New Year's too."

"Don't let her take you away from your new bride-to-be." Chase Rawlston had recently asked Zoe Jenkins to marry him after a harrowing case that brought the two of them and her little baby girl together. This would be their first Christmas as a couple, and that took precedence over work. Considering Chase's tragic loss of his wife and child in DC five years ago, they both deserved this time together. Cara should show more empathy, given what Chase had been through.

Chase laughed. "Well, Cara is my boss, and by the sounds of it, I'll probably be inviting her to dinner."

Sully's stomach bottomed out like a rock.

Chase had to be mistaken. "I hope you're not saying that Cara is planning a trip out west, are you?"

Silence ensued. "Um… I assumed she told you."

"She hasn't called me since before she went into surgery." Sully left out the fact that she was unconscious the last time he spoke to her. "I told her there was no point in coming out here. Did she say when?"

"Yes, she called me to tell me she was taking the first plane out in the morning. This visit isn't out of the ordinary. She flies in all the time. She was just here at Thanksgiving after the RMK arrest. You know that. You were there."

Sully remembered being in the same room with her all too well. They barely said two words to each other. "Fine, but she was just stabbed. The anesthesia hasn't even worn off yet. She needs to heal. Did she tell you why she was flying out here?" As if Sully didn't know.

"Does she need a reason? She *is* in charge of MCK9. Why are you so upset about this?"

"Because I know she isn't coming here for an inspection of your work. She's coming here to inspect *mine*."

Cara stepped out of the jetway with Mocha beside her. After the dog's keen detection at the training facility, Cara wanted to give her some extra attention and training. Cara also felt better with having a K-9 by her side in case Morel sent another one of his soldiers after her. To burn her trail, Cara bought two tickets, one to California and one to Wyoming. She sent her assistant to California with the ticket in Cara's name. Tracy bore an uncanny resemblance to her with the same short black hair. Whereas Cara's eyes were green, Tracy's blues needed contacts and a pair of crystal-framed eyeglasses to finish the disguise. Tracy would appear in LA and quickly return to DC. By the time Morel realized Tracy wasn't Cara, Cara hoped to be already on her way to her sister's house, and Tracy's protection detail would make sure she made it back safely as well. Cara exited to the passenger pickup area and spotted the MCK9 SUV waiting for her at the curb. Chase had come through in picking her up.

Gingerly pulling her luggage behind her with one hand and holding Mocha's leash with the other, she approached the black vehicle from behind. As she neared it, the passenger window lowered.

"Thanks for picking me up." She approached the door. Only it wasn't Chase behind the wheel. It was Sully. She stopped short of opening the door. "What are you doing here?"

"I should ask you the same question, and it's nice to see you too. Why aren't you in a hospital?" He didn't wait for an answer, as if she owed him one. He opened his door to step to the back of the vehicle. Pulling the hatch wide, he revealed two dog crates, one occupied.

"Mocha, in," she commanded. As her dog settled inside the crate, Cara said, "I see you still have Deacon. He must be getting on in years." The sleek, black Doberman pinscher raised an eyebrow at her. Cara gave him a brief smile.

"He's a dependable dog. We work well

together. He's devoted and in it for the long haul. Ending our relationship for no reason doesn't feel right."

Cara eyed Sully with a sideways glance. She noticed his brown hair graying at the temples, but other than that, Sully, at fifty-three, was still in prime shape. She ignored his dig, obviously meant for her, and said, "Since when do US Marshals drive K-9 unit vehicles? And where is Chase?"

Sully closed the rear doors and headed back to the driver's seat. "Chase had a prior engagement with Zoe's family. I offered to pick you up. I took his vehicle so you could easily find me." He settled in behind the wheel, leaving Cara with no other alternatives. "Are you coming or not?"

Suddenly, a loud noise echoed from behind. The blast sounded like a gunshot, and Cara dropped to her knees. Pain shot from her shoulder wound on the impact and the next thing she knew, Sully was beside her.

"Hey, it was just an old truck backfiring." His face leaned close and his intense, hawklike eyes she remembered well leveled on her. For a moment, she let herself catch her breath. Then she pushed herself up and away from him. "At least let me help you up," he said.

"I got myself down here. I'll get myself up." She gritted her teeth as she used her good arm for leverage. She was on her feet and inside the car before Sully moved from his spot.

When he stood, he leaned in through the opened window, once again coming close to her. She faced forward but could feel his warm breath on her cheek.

"Why are you here, Cara?" he whispered. "You know there is nothing you can do for Jeanette. Nothing has changed in ten years. Nothing will ever change. What do you hope to accomplish by this impromptu trip?"

She slowly turned his way. She knew he was right but couldn't tell him that. He'd always been right to keep her in the dark. "I have to know that she's safe. That's all. No one has to know that I checked on her. And Jeanette will never see me."

The intensity in his eyes softened. "Aw, Cara. Jeanette is alive and well and loves the life that was created for her. She's happy, believe me. She's safe and spends her days painting, just as you wanted. You know if you see her, you risk her losing all of that."

"I want to speak with her handler. Once I'm satisfied that he's up for the task, I'll go."

Sully's gaze averted from hers. The shift happened so quickly that she knew something was wrong. "It's not possible." He moved away from the window and circled around the front of the truck to the driver's side. Putting the vehicle into gear, Sully drove off from the pickup area in silence.

"You never were a good liar, so you might as well tell the truth. You haven't heard from her handler, have you?"

Sully took the highway entrance to Elk Valley, glancing her way with his mouth open to respond. After a moment, he closed it and shook his head. "Just let me do my job, Cara. This doesn't concern you."

"We'll see about that."

THREE

Ten minutes in Cara's company and Sully remembered why they never would have made it as a couple. Her distrust in him never made sense. He used to take it personally, thought that if he tried a little harder, then maybe next time, he would get it right. But that next time never came. And eventually, she walked out on him without even a backward glance.

"I'll be heading to Jeanette's," he told her. "If there's a problem, you'll be the first to know."

"So does that mean she's nearby?"

Sully held his tongue from saying more, not wanting to give away Jeanette's location.

"I'm going with you."

Sully shook his head and took the turn

into the Mountain Country K-9 Unit head-quarters. He pulled into Chase's designated spot and cut the engine.

"You know that's not possible. For once, you're going to have to trust me to do my job."

She sent a heated gaze his way. "For once? I trusted you for ten years with Jeanette's life. It's not you I don't trust, it's Morel. He's coming for her."

"He'll never find her. She's in the most remote area, with nothing around for miles. And by the way, your decision to leave the hospital and come here contradicts your claim of trusting me." Sully observed the building. "I filled everyone in. They're going to keep you safe while I investigate the matter."

"I'm not the one with the target on my back. I can't involve the people at the unit in this. That's letting too many people in on Jeanette's whereabouts. If Morel learned that anyone at the MCK9 knew where my sister was, all their lives would be at risk. I'm not dumb, Sully. I know how to keep people safe."

"Everyone but yourself, you mean." He stepped from the vehicle and retrieved Deacon from his cage. Cara guided Mocha out as well. Sully slammed the doors. "Go inside and have some eggnog. Enjoy the holidays with your team. Celebrate their victory over finding the Rocky Mountain Killer this year. Make yourself comfortable because you're not going anywhere."

Sully made his way to his own vehicle, an unmarked SUV, and loaded up Deacon in his crate. A glance back at Cara showed she'd followed his orders. He saw no sight of her or her dog. Sully figured she must've gone inside, and he climbed behind his wheel. He tried Logan one more time before hitting the road.

"Pick up." Frustration set in. Why would Logan Doyle choose this time to go AWOL? The man would lose his job unless he had a real good reason for stepping off his post.

Sully pulled out onto the road, preparing for his seven-hour drive west. He thought of the quaint ranch he had put Jeanette on, going above his duty to give her a nice new life. He took the ribbing for playing favorites, not caring what his colleagues said. All that mattered was that Cara's sacrifice of giving up the only family she had would have a silver lining.

Snowflakes hit his windshield, light at first but soon requiring the wipers. He turned the radio on and listened to the mindless chatter of the hosts as the snow picked up. Any worse and his trip would double in time. If the weather worsened, the roads might even close completely. He thought about calling Logan again, but he needed to focus on driving.

A few cars pulled off to the side of the road, unable to pass through. He drove by them in his four-wheel-drive vehicle and glanced in his rearview mirror. Another SUV drove behind him a short distance away. He recognized the vehicle instantly. It appeared Cara hadn't gone inside the MCK9 building after all. Rather, she climbed back into Chase's SUV and now tailed him.

Sully chuckled, knowing that if he didn't laugh, he might just shout in anger.

"What do you want from me, Cara?" he

spoke aloud into the cabin of his vehicle, having a notion of turning around.

He already knew the answer. She wanted him to lead her to her sister. But at what cost? If he drove on, he could lose his job. If he didn't, he could lose Cara.

I already lost her.

The thought echoed in his mind. He may have lost a future with Cara by his side, but the two of them had found a way to coexist amicably in their lines of work.

Sort of.

He watched the vehicle pull back and chuckled. She knew he was onto her.

He had to give her credit. Cara was fantastic at her job. And she was the most responsible person he'd ever known. Perhaps he could lead her to Jeanette just this once, let her see from afar that her sister was happy and safe. Cara may struggle to trust him, but in this moment, he trusted Cara would do the right thing later.

Sully slowed down a bit to give her time to catch back up again. Soon, the two of them drove on at a comfortable pace. It felt almost companionable, as though they traveled together. This little game they played could be disastrous, but it could also end beautifully.

Sully imagined the look on Cara's face when she saw her sister again. He grinned ear to ear, his reflection in the mirror as dopey as ever.

Then he caught sight of another vehicle speeding up to pass Cara, and his smile slipped from his face. A black four-door sedan moved dangerously close to Chase's SUV. It stopped at Cara's window and moved in closer.

The driver didn't mean to pass her. He meant to hit her.

Cara's vehicle jolted to the right, the steering wheel slipping in her hands. Through the snow hitting her windshield, she saw Sully bring his SUV to a stop in front of her at the same moment.

It took Cara a moment to realize that someone had hit her. A glance out her driver's window showed a black sedan coming too close. Metal against metal collided again before she could move out of the way.

Maintaining control of her car took precedence. One more hit like that and she could end up in the ditch. She didn't dare take her eyes off the road, but she also couldn't remain in this vulnerable spot. With Sully stopped up ahead, Cara sped up and yanked her wheel to the left to take the next turn by surprise.

"Call Chase Rawlston," she stated, directing her phone to make the call through Bluetooth. After two rings, he picked up.

"Is everything all right, boss?" his voice spoke through the vehicle's speakers.

"I'm going to need backup. I followed Sully, heading west. Now I have someone trying to push me off the road." Cara had known Sully was onto her. He wasn't a top US Marshal for no reason. She just didn't expect him to realize she'd tailed him so soon. Now she was glad he had. She glanced in her rearview mirror to see if Sully had followed her.

"Did you get a good look at the driver?"

"It's snowing too hard. I did everything I could just to get out of his path." She gave him the make and model of the car, keeping the man in her rearview mirror.

Sully was nowhere in sight.

"Did you get that?" she asked when Chase hadn't responded.

Still no response.

"Chase?" She sighed when she realized the connection was lost. "Great. Now I'm out here in the middle of the prairie with nothing but my sidearm, an unruly K-9 in the back and a beat-up SUV."

SUV. A plan formed.

Cara's vehicle, even damaged, would stand up against the weather better than a sedan. She may need to take this thing off-roading.

Removing her weapon from her side holster, Cara placed it within quick and easy reach. She picked up her speed, hoping to give herself a cushion. A forest of thick trees came into view around a bend. As soon as Cara reached the outskirts, she drove off the road and down into the thick of them. Turning the wheel, she came to a stop, grabbed her gun and flung open the door. She raced to the rear of the SUV and released Mocha from her crate. She grabbed Chase's bag of ammunition and removed enough bullets to make her point with this man.

"Stay." The command had Mocha sitting at the ready while Cara settled in behind her car door with her gun at eye level.

The sedan raced in, following her tracks off the road, bumping along the unpaved portion. The uneven terrain and weather didn't seem to bother her pursuer. She understood he had a job to do and his own boss to answer to. Cara needed to send a clear message back to Morel, one that told him he'd messed with the wrong woman. If he thought she would be as naive and controllable as Jeanette, he would learn today that he was wrong. Cara had devoted her life to being the one in charge. No one could hurt her when she was at the top.

Including this goon.

Morel would learn fast that if he wanted to deal with her, he would have to do it himself. At least make the playing field equal. She may have been caught off guard yesterday, but it wouldn't happen again. That was his one given.

"Stand down!" Cara ordered the man as he jumped from his vehicle with his gun in his hand.

He took three shots as his answer.

That was all Cara needed to unload her own.

The passenger door of the car opened, and a second shooter appeared, firing rapidly. Mocha whined from behind her. Cara wasn't ready to send her out into the spray of bullets. One command to bite should be enough for a K-9 to apprehend the assailant. But relying on Mocha to act without hesitancy wasn't possible. Fear could get her killed.

Cara reloaded her gun, staying low behind her door. Bullets pelted off the side of the SUV as she took aim.

One bullet hit the first shooter's thigh. Her second hit his arm, and he dropped the gun. The other assailant ran closer to her, shooting haphazardly.

She heard the pop of her tires and knew she wouldn't be going anywhere in this car. They could take out her tires, but they wouldn't be taking her out. She reloaded again. But before she could lift her gun, another gun blasted from behind her and the second assailant fell to the ground, dead.

The first shooter raced back to the car and spun his wheels to get out. He made it back up the embankment and slipped and slid all the way down the road in his escape.

Silence fell over the scene as Cara looked around to see who had taken the death shot.

One moment she saw no one around, but in the next, Sully stepped out of the trees, his gun at his side.

With less than twenty feet between them, she locked gazes with him. The anger in his intense eyes spoke volumes. *Go home, Cara.*

She shook her head.

"It's too late. I won't go until I see her with my own eyes." But with Chase's SUV now undrivable, Sully wouldn't just lead her to Jeanette. Sully would take her to her sister.

FOUR

Sully stepped away from the local law enforcement who were processing the scene. He'd been given the all-clear to continue with his plans and trip to Jackson. Halfway between the scene and where he parked his car, he stopped in indecision. Ahead, he could see Cara standing by his vehicle, talking on her phone. Her strict mannerisms and body language showed her level of power. She most likely was giving the MCK9 unit her orders and laying out her own plans, which conflicted with his own. As he stood on this middle ground, he felt himself wavering in his position. The thought dumbfounded him. He had never been double-minded.

Sully called on his beliefs, digging deep to where he held tightly to the word of God,

Scriptures hidden in his heart for moments such as these. He drew on the promise that God had not given him a spirit of apprehension. God gives a sound mind, power and love.

But then, had God known Cara Haines would come into his life and disrupt everything? It was as though the two of them picked up where they'd left off ten years ago. Who would be in charge? It was all-or-nothing for her.

Sully began the trek toward her, mentally preparing reasons for her to return to the MCK9 and let him do his job. But when he stepped up in front of her, she clicked off the phone and began a whole briefing of everything she'd set in motion with her team. All Sully could do was stand and listen with no way to get a word in edge-wise.

"Are you listening to me?" she asked.

"I'm hearing everything you're saying," he said. "And I'm hearing everything you're not saying."

"What's that supposed to mean?"

"The fact that this is not your jurisdiction. I don't work for you. I am a United States

Marshal, and the witness protection program falls under my responsibility."

Cara's eyes widened behind her glasses. "Excuse me, but I was attacked...twice. The current threat takes precedence over witness security from ten years ago. These are crimes in progress that must be stopped."

"So does this mean you'll return to the MCK9 and handle these crimes?"

"I have my team working on it. Chase is pulling in as many of the local officers who are available. They can handle things in Elk Valley and the vicinity around."

"I had a feeling you would say that." Why was saying no to her so difficult? *Just say it.*

She turned and opened the passenger door, stepping a foot inside while the word hung on his tongue.

No.

"Are you coming, or should I drive?" She stopped halfway in the car, leveling her stare of authority at him as if he was a low-level rookie.

Frustration set in. *I have a sound mind.* He repeated this promise quietly to himself with a deep breath. "Why are you doing this? Why can't you trust me to handle this and make sure Jennie is safe?"

"Jennie? That's her new name? You couldn't even change her first name to something like Wanda, or something vastly different? Why don't you just drop a pin on a map so Luis can track her right down?"

"I gave her the name she wanted. I did everything you asked me to do. By you going to see her now, it'll all be for nothing. There's no guarantee I can get her this life again. Right now, she's safe. Do you really want to risk everything?"

"I could ask you the same question. Deep down, you know you could be wrong. Do you really want to risk her life? Now get in the car and drive." She climbed the rest of the way in and shut the door. He watched her put her seat belt on. Then she raised her slender wrist and tapped her watch.

A sudden laugh escaped his lips. Did she just tap her watch at him? His first thought was if she was serious. But he didn't have to think too long. Cara was always serious.

He felt his smile slip from his face. He

wasn't sure he'd ever heard Cara laugh in all the time they dated. Had her tough exterior been from more than the badge she wore?

But there was one time he caught her smiling.

Sully moved around the front of his SUV and climbed in behind the wheel. Even as he started the engine, he questioned his reasoning. Cara had him second-guessing himself. Was he caving into her demands because of his doubts about Jennie's safety? Or was it because everything he'd ever done for Cara was for the hope of seeing her smile again?

In the back of the SUV, Mocha jumped in the crate while Deacon remained still and poised. Cara sighed as she stared out the window, watching a snowy Wyoming drift by. Five hours in, and she didn't know where Sully was driving to. He remained as still as his dog.

And silent.

Cara needed to break the tension somehow. She knew he had a protocol to follow. She knew all about those rules, every painful one of them. Cara reminded herself daily of those rules, and even as she moved closer to her sister's location, she knew she couldn't breach them.

"I'm not sure Mocha will make it as a K-9," she spoke the first thing that came to mind, but not what was really in her heart.

The dog whined at the sound of her name, proving Cara's statement about her.

Sully glanced in the rearview mirror before shrugging. "Perhaps not, but I'm glad to see you not giving up on her so easily."

He was back to his passive remarks about the dogs that weren't really about the dogs. Cara weighed her words carefully. Regardless of their past and how things had been left between them, she would remain professional throughout this trip. Their relationship had been ten years ago. It was time for him to get over it.

"What you see as giving up, I see as what's best for all parties," she said. "There are good reasons for goodbyes."

He put his turn signal on and took the next exit. She glanced around the wide-open terrain for a sign of their location. Was this the town where Jeanette lived? Before she could ask, he said, "As long as both parties have a say. Otherwise, it's giving up."

Cara faced him directly, ready to deny his accusation. She took a deep breath instead. "And how would you like me to ask Mocha about her wishes? She doesn't have a say because she can't talk."

He shrugged again and pulled into a rest area with fast-food restaurants. He parked in front of a dog area. "Maybe relinquishing some of your control and demands so she can show you she's worth the effort. She's a dog, not a robot. If she truly wants to please you, she'll do it without command. It's part of the trust you build with her, not order from her. You used to be an amazing K-9 trainer. How could you have forgotten this crucial component?"

Cara readied to deny his accusation but held her tongue. She questioned if he was right. Did taking the DC job cause a lapse in her training skills, or had her choice to leave training for a desk job been more about her unwillingness to loosen the leash?

In more ways than one.

She opened the door to retrieve Mocha. At the back with doors opened, Cara clipped the leash onto the K-9's vest collar. Circling the leash around her wrist, Cara guided the dog down and toward the dog area. She stood away from Sully and Deacon as though they didn't know each other. But it wasn't true. Sully knew all about her. In a lapse of judgment during a night while they dated, Cara spilled all about her past to the man. Jeanette had just married Luis and found out about the monster he was. Cara remembered feeling as though she'd lost all control over her life with no way to protect her sister. Cara had broken down and pleaded with Sully to help, and before she knew what she was doing, she'd told him everything. She vowed to never make herself so vulnerable again. It was a moment of weakness that became a wedge between them after that night. The strong and fearless woman she portrayed to the world was proved to be false. And Sully knew it. But then Sully knew everything, even things she wasn't allowed to know.

And that was the heart of the matter.

Cara moved to return Mocha to the vehicle. "Crate."

"Wait," Sully called from behind, halting Cara in mid-step. When she turned his way, he held a red rubber ball in his hand. "When was the last time someone played with her?"

Cara scoffed. "There's no time for that. We need to get back on the road. Who knows who's on our tail as we speak?"

"Then all the more reason to make sure she'll be there when you need her." Before she knew what he was about to do, he threw the ball at her.

It hit her on the cheek and fell to the ground.

Cara pursed her lips. "I don't think you're funny."

"I can't believe you didn't catch that." His eyes danced with suppressed laughter. He walked toward her and picked up the ball. This time, he placed it in her hand. "Play with her. It's the best way to build trust."

"If this will get us back on the road, fine." Cara released the leash from Mocha's vest. She pulled back her arm and let the ball sail through the air. Sully held Deacon in place, commanding him to stay. Mocha glanced at the ball and back at Cara. A look of longing in her black eyes mixed with confusion irked Cara. She hadn't expected for Sully to be proved right over something as silly as a game of fetch. "Go. Fetch."

Mocha took one tentative step, then picked up her pace until she was in a fullblown run. She swooped down and, in her open slack jaws, scooped up the ball and stopped. With the ball in her mouth, she glanced at Cara, but didn't return.

"Get down on your knees," Sully said. "Lower to her level and hold out your hand."

The whole thing seemed ridiculous. This was a working dog. Treating her like this could ruin her completely as a K-9. And yet, Cara bent down on her knees.

Slowly, Mocha approached her, both of them broaching unfamiliar territory. She dropped the ball a foot away from Cara.

When Cara moved to reach for it, Sully stopped her.

"Tell her to fetch it," he whispered. "And bring it to you."

Cara understood why Sully wanted her to carry this through. But what if Mocha didn't complete the task? What if it was too late to earn trust because Mocha failed crucial training to be a K-9 officer?

"Fetch the ball and bring it to me," Cara ordered.

Mocha tilted her head, then lowered it to the ground to scoop up the ball again. This time, she took the remaining steps and placed the ball into Cara's waiting hands. The dog stepped back, but Cara reached out and tussled her fur quickly for reinforcement.

Suddenly, Mocha raced up to Cara, huffing in satisfaction. She slobbered a bit on Cara's cheek.

As Cara tried to avoid the dog's tongue, she said, "Now I fear she's really ruined."

When Sully didn't respond, Cara looked up at him. A strange expression filled his eyes as he watched her intently. Just as quickly as the look had come, it disappeared, and he turned toward the SUV.

"Let's get the dogs back inside and we'll grab some food before heading out."

Cara followed him to the vehicle and once the dogs were secure, she and Sully went into the rest area.

Sully held the door for her, and Cara paused before entering. "When I'm wrong, I say I'm wrong. And I might have been wrong with Mocha."

"Might have?" Laughter filled his voice.

"Time will tell," she said, passing through the door.

The interior of the rest area was bright and cheery. Someone had painted a mural on the far wall that depicted beautiful Jackson Hole. Ski slopes overlooked the quaint Western town that Cara remembered fondly from when she lived in the state and frequented the town. Slowly, she approached the wall, taking in the stunning image.

"It's beautiful. Seems wrong to be at a rest stop." Cara walked along the painting, studying every fine detail from the bear on the mountaintop to the child's face on the ski slope. Twinkling lights warmed the downtown. As Cara came to the end of the mural, she found the artist's signature.

Jennie.

She thought back to when Sully had called Jeanette Jennie, but it had to be a coincidence. This couldn't be her sister's work. Her sister was in hiding. She would be foolish to be commissioning her skills.

But when Cara turned and faced Sully, the shocked expression on his face told her he knew who the artist was as well.

"Did you authorize this?"

He shook his head. "She was only supposed to paint for herself. That was the deal. Her handler knows this."

"The handler who is MIA? It seems to me your man isn't doing his job. Which means neither are you."

FIVE

"Why am I not surprised your sister would go against the rules?" Sully asked around the last bite of a cheap burrito. It was the fastest food available because they needed to get back on the road. He climbed in behind the wheel and started the engine. He hit the windshield wipers to swipe away the accumulating snow that had built up while they were inside the rest stop. "After everything I did to make sure she was safe. What was she thinking? She might as well have posted a neon sign on the ranch that said, 'Here I am. Come and get me.'"

"I'm glad to see you're finally believing Jeanette's in danger," Cara said smugly from the passenger seat. "Or I guess it's Jennie now." Cara buckled up. "No more denying the facts. Call in backup."

Sully drove out of the parking lot. "For what?" He sped up and reentered the highway. "I never said I believed she was in danger. I still don't think her identity's been breached. The only threats have been on you."

"Then what's the hurry?" Cara leveled her self-assured gaze at him.

Sully let off the gas a bit. He nearly growled at her keen awareness. He'd let her see his worry. For a moment, he drove through the storm in silence, considering his next move. He could call in his team, but under what evidence? At two days before Christmas and a snowstorm, he doubted that would go over well.

"I'm eager to have a few choice words with Logan, that's all," Sully said. "The marshal shouldn't have allowed her to take her painting so public. It was only supposed to be a pastime."

"My sister has always been an artist. It's all she ever wanted to be."

"You coddled her. You still are. If she's in danger, she brought it on herself."

"I protected her. There's a difference.

Something Logan is failing to do. But it looks like he's not the only one." An underlying threat laced Cara's insinuating words.

"I have always protected her, just as you asked. You can't keep sacrificing your life for her." Sully huffed and took the next exit.

"Sacrificing my life? I didn't give up my life for her."

"No, you gave up the life *we* had." Sully cringed, wishing he could inhale those words back in.

Cara faced forward in silence. Her eyes drifted closed, and she dropped her head back on the headrest. "I thought we were past this, Sully. It wouldn't have worked anyway. *We* wouldn't have worked."

"Funny, I don't remember weighing in on that discussion."

"There was no point. I made the decision."

"Right. And your opinion is the only one that matters."

"Yes." Her response was blunt and cut deep. But he wasn't surprised.

Sully took another turn, but the snow accumulation made the side roads difficult to navigate. The tires spun a bit and slipped around. The number of trees picked up, and the forest grew denser with each mile toward the secluded ranch tucked in a small mountain town.

The snowfall picked up, making visibility near zero. Sully slowed the SUV, trying to see the road ahead.

Suddenly, a loud crack echoed through the air. He strained to see where it had come from.

"Stop the car!" Cara shouted. She raised her arms over her head.

Sully hit the brakes, skidding, still uncertain what she had seen. Then a louder crack, followed by a large tree crashing down directly in front of them, had him gripping the steering wheel even as he knew they were in a slide. The distance between his SUV and the tree lessened by the second.

"Hold on!" The moment of impact sent his SUV to a jarring stop with a portion of his truck jammed above the trunk of the tree and the rest on a perilous angle. Any amount of gas he applied only spun the wheels, going nowhere. The heavy thud of the tree trunk falling still shook his bones.

And frazzled his nerves.

The dogs barked in unison and jumped in their crates.

"Down," Sully commanded as he sat in shock over the sight before him. If he hadn't listened to Cara, they would be dead.

Dead.

"This was the third attempt on your life," he said.

"Or the heavy snow brought it down."

"You don't really believe that, do you?" He felt his eyes widen in disbelief at her silly notion. She couldn't be serious.

Cara turned his way, and he expected her to fight him on this too. Instead, she simply said, "No. Someone wants us dead. Someone who knows our location. We're being hunted."

"No, not us. Someone wants *you* dead."

"How much farther to Jeanette's?" Cara asked after observing the fallen tree across the road. Even if they could get the tree off the truck, the undercarriage of the vehicle was clearly damaged. Various fluids leaked out onto the pristine snow. But these were still better than their spilled blood.

"I can't just walk up to the ranch," Sully said while trying to push the vehicle off the tree trunk. He strained with no amount of budging from the car.

"You're wasting your energy. We need to get a lay of the land and find the closest residents. If not Jeanette's ranch, then someone else's."

"There is no one else around here. It's why I chose this place. She would be in complete isolation."

Cara folded her arms, a bit out of annoyance but more out of the cold setting in. "Witness protection wasn't supposed to isolate her. It was supposed to reinsert her back into society with a new life. How is living out here all alone doing that?"

"Morel has people everywhere. And she isn't all alone. It's an artist colony. People come for various lengths of residence to work on their artwork. She was among her own people. She chose this. I made her the owner and permanent resident."

Cara cocked her head, considering his words. "I suppose that sounded like a dream to Jeanette. It would have been what she always wanted." Cara knew she should thank him, but they weren't out of the woods yet. Jeanette's new life would most likely be uprooted after today. "I see how a breach of her new life could ruin this for her."

His eyes widened, and he stepped down off the trunk. "It's a little late for that."

Cara frowned, understanding his reason for wanting her to stay behind. But he was right; there was no going back now. She avoided his stare and approached the base of the tree trunk about ten feet from the side of the road. Cara figured the tree to be at least three feet wide at its base. She inspected the wood and saw no decay inside its bark. The tree had been alive and well.

A scan of the snow around the base displayed evidence of someone cutting the tree down. Sawdust showed through the first layer of snow even as more flakes fell from the sky. And though the newly fallen snow-covered footprints, the evidence of a pair of large men's boots trailed off into the woods.

"Our lumberjack went this way." Cara pointed.

"We're not going that way. First, he most likely wants us to follow him, and it could be an ambush. Second, we don't have much time out here if we want to stay alive. The sun is going down and we have nothing but the coats on our backs to keep us warm."

"But if we go to the ranch, we'll lead him right to Jeanette."

"We have the dogs. They'll alert us to his presence."

"Deacon, maybe. I doubt Mocha is up to that task."

"Alerting is a requirement for a K-9," Sully said as he approached the rear of the vehicle and opened the door.

Cara followed him. "You don't have to tell me twice. Taking her on this trip was my last-ditch effort to train her."

"There's a chance she becomes a liability instead."

"Are you suggesting we leave her here?"

"That would be cruel on our part." He reached into Mocha's crate and rubbed the black fur by her nose, lifting her gaze to his. "Sit."

Mocha sat back on her haunches with a little huff. Her breath puffed to vapor in the cold.

Sully opened a backpack and removed booties for the dogs' paws. "She's following commands. I think she'll be okay." He passed a set to Cara while he fitted Deacon into his boots.

"Down," Sully said, and both dogs jumped out. "Guard," he gave, issuing the next command, and headed in the opposite direction of the footprints.

"Is it far?" Cara asked.

Sully didn't respond right away. She realized he had an ear turned to their surroundings, and she took his unspoken command to walk in silence. Knowing the distance wasn't important. Getting there alive was.

Two hours passed by, and Deacon whined and alerted to his right. Mocha followed Deacon and did the same. Sully put his arm up to stop Cara, jerking his head to the right and nodding to the left. He wanted her to go left behind a wide tree.

Cara frowned and instead removed her gun from inside her coat. As she gripped the pistol, she noticed her fingers struggled to clench it. They were stiff from the cold temperatures.

"Are you all right?" Sully whispered.

"I don't need to be coddled. I'm a trained FBI agent who can handle her own." She tightened her fingers and lifted the weapon. Her wounded shoulder said otherwise, but she kept that to herself.

"Fine. He's cutting us off. We'll need to take the longer route if we're going to avoid him."

"Why don't we just apprehend him?" Cara heard the exasperation in her voice.

"And then what? Take him with us? I'd like to avoid that until we have backup. We need to get to the ranch first."

Cara didn't like leaving this man free to continue to hunt them, but with each moment, the sky darkened, and they needed to find shelter.

"Come," she called to Mocha.

But instead of responding to the command, Mocha only had eyes for Deacon.

Cara glanced at Sully to see if he noticed and, at his nod, he directed Deacon in the opposite direction. Mocha immediately followed.

Interesting. Perhaps there was hope for the dog yet.

With the K-9s at the lead, Cara and Sully fell in behind them, each with their weapon in their hand. The terrain rose in elevation on this alternative route. An icy wind picked up at the higher elevation. Cara's work boots didn't hold up to the deep snow. At some point, she realized she couldn't feel her feet any longer. Her hand also stuck to her gun.

"Frostbite is setting in," she whispered. She heard a strange sound coming from her voice. "Am I slurring my words?" She hoped it was her imagination, but then, if she hallucinated, that wouldn't be good either.

"It's not much farther. I think," Sully replied. "I've never walked these woods, but I'm pretty sure we're coming in from the rear of the property. I hope anyway."

Cara realized he put an arm around her shoulders and pulled her close to him, but she couldn't feel him. She leaned in, knowing something was wrong, but she struggled to form the words to say it.

No, she didn't want to say it. The idea of admitting to a weakness made her want to scream in frustration. She should be able to hold her own. Even more, she should be able to be in charge. She was the big boss. She'd earned that title for a reason. Admitting defeat now would make everything a lie.

It would make her a liar and a fraud.

Heat scorched her cheeks and neck. She pulled at her collar and stumbled.

"Cara?" Sully's voice seemed so far away, not mere inches. "I got you. Stay awake."

Cara jolted and thought she had fallen asleep on her feet. Except she wasn't walking anymore. For a moment, she realized she was being carried. How long had she fallen asleep for? Before she could ask, darkness overtook her completely.

SIX

Finally, the outline of the barn came into view beneath the moonlit sky. They'd made it to the ranch. But were they too late?

Sully glanced down into Cara's unconscious face as the dogs walked on either side of him, keeping guard. This was his own fault. He should have locked her up to keep her safe. But he couldn't deal with the what-ifs right now. He needed to get her someplace warm and revive her.

He passed by the barn and neared the single-story ranch house. All lights were off, and no one looked home. The sight boiled his blood. If they came all this way for nothing, risking their lives, Logan would pay for it. Moving the witness without permission was against protocol. Logan knew he needed to inform Sully if Jennie needed to be moved to a safe house. "I'll have his badge," Sully said desperately as he trudged through the knee-deep snow toward the house.

A sound came from behind just as Deacon alerted to it. How had the dog not heard sooner?

Sully had no time to figure it out. He picked up his steps and trudged through the snow at a fast clip, spraying the loose powder all around. The back door loomed ahead, feeling forever out of reach.

A gunshot blasted through the night, its bullet banging off the roofline. Sully turned to the left and then the right. Back and forth, he evaded the gun's scope. Bullets sprayed the surrounding snow, and then one took him down. Hot, searing pain emanated from his back, but he pushed up onto his knees and targeted the last five feet to the door.

A moan escaped Cara's lips as he placed her on the threshold, her back against the wooden door. He tried the doorknob, and it turned. He caught Cara before she fell into the house.

"Inside," he commanded the dogs, and they ran in behind him. He pulled Cara the rest of the way through and slammed the door, locking it. "Hang in there, Cara." He tapped her frozen cheek to wake her up. Taking her hands, he tried to warm them by rubbing them with his own. He was also too cold to make a difference.

"Please, God, don't let me be too late."

Staying low, Sully carried her closer to a heating vent. Thankfully, hot air poured forth. Placing her by it, he scanned the room for a blanket. A sofa about ten feet away had one folded neatly on the top.

"Guard her," he ordered Deacon, and crawled over to the sofa. He had to stand to get it, and as soon as he did, a bullet blasted through the window and landed in the wall above the sofa.

Sully dropped to the floor with the blanket and crawled back to Cara. He wrapped her tightly with the wool, realizing she was already coming to. Her eyes fluttered before closing again.

"We're at the ranch, but no one's here," he whispered. He looked around the wide-open space. "At least I don't think so. I need to search the place to find out if we're alone inside. We have company outside."

Cara trembled fiercely, and he tucked the blanket up to her chin, staying close to her and rubbing her frozen hands. He was glad to see her trembling again. When she had stopped, he knew hypothermia was setting in. Living his whole life in Wyoming, he'd seen enough people succumb to the cold to know the signs. He also knew the slow and steady warmth would revive her. Sully would just rather not have a predator outside waiting to take them out. He needed to eradicate that threat as well.

He also needed to tend to his own wound. Feeling around his back, he felt the place his skin burned. From what he could tell, the bullet only grazed his side and the pain he experienced was probably more of a bruised or broken rib than anything else.

As Cara awakened further, he leaned close to study her eyes. He looked for coherency. But what he found was disappointment.

"I did my best," he said as she turned her face away from his.

"But I didn't," she replied. "I was nothing but an anchor for you. If we die here tonight, it'll be my fault. Not yours."

"That's not going to happen. Guard," he ordered Deacon. Pushing back, he took his gun into his hand and said, "Mocha, come."

Cara tried to sit up. "No. Don't take her. Leave her with me and take Deacon."

"You're not in charge of this one." He held the gun up. "Stay here and warm up. And stay low."

"Sully, you can't let the shooter leave here. He'll go right to Morel and tell him of this location."

"You got it, boss." And with that, he slipped out into the dark night, now the hunter himself.

I can't stay here like a useless lump. Cara forced herself to sit up, still clutching the blanket to her trembling body. Her skin burned and ached as feeling seeped back in. Knowing Sully needed backup and his dog pushed her to her knees. If she thought she could stand without falling on her face, she would go out there to help him.

But I've done enough damage already.

As Cara moved away from her spot, her hand encountered a sticky substance. In the darkness, she couldn't see what she touched, but she recognized the feel.

Blood.

She knew she wasn't cut, which meant the blood belonged to Mocha or Sully. Judging by the way Mocha left with no symptoms of being hurt, it could only have been Sully.

More guilt flooded through Cara. *He's hurt because of me. But then I always caused his hurt.* Nothing had changed as far as she could tell. She was still a hazard to him. The best thing she could do was to organize her team here as fast as possible.

Figuring Sully would not have put Jeanette in a place with no way to contact her, there had to be a satellite phone somewhere. From her coat pocket, she withdrew her own useless cell phone to use as a flashlight. Making her way toward the kitchen, she crawled along smooth wood floors. Shadows of Jeanette's artwork lined the walls above her. From what Cara could see, the home was pristine with her sister's artistic touches everywhere. She'd filled even the kitchen with everything a gourmet chef could ask for. Stainless steel appliances and stone counters made for a wonderful artistic retreat. Cara envisioned her sister hosting many artists over the last ten years. She must have been in her glory.

All because of Sully.

He really outdid himself, providing more than what Cara had asked of him. *Take care of her, give her a good life, one she can love forever.* He had done just that.

All the while saying goodbye to her.

Don't leave me, Cara! His words still haunted her. She may have left him ten years ago, but she would not leave him now.

Slowly, she made it to her knees. Just as she had thought, a satellite phone sat at a desk against the far wall of the kitchen. She shut her flashlight off and crept slowly through the dark. But before she made it to the desk, she slipped and fell to her face. Her hands landed in more blood.

Too much blood.

How was Sully still standing? He had to be bleeding out with this much blood loss. And now he was out in the freezing cold. Even if Morel's man didn't get Sully, a wound like this would kill him.

Cara crawled through the huge puddle of blood and made it to the desk. She reached up for the phone and made the call to Chase.

"Where are you?" he asked.

Cara gave him the directions Sully had taken to get here. "But the road is closed. A tree fell on us. You're going to have to helicopter in. It's the only house in the area. You shouldn't have any trouble getting to us. Fast, Chase. Sully is badly hurt."

"I'll get our team out there as soon as possible. I'll also have Ian chopper in from Montana. He's a lot closer to you than I am."

One of the K-9 officers, Ian Carpenter, lived in Cattle Bend, Montana, staying there after he became engaged to Meadow. He now covered that territory for the MCK9 Unit.

"Do you have this number in case you need to reach me?" Cara asked.

"Yes. I have it on my caller ID. Stay safe. We're on our way." Chase ended the call and Cara sat back against the wall with the phone in her lap. She turned on her cell phone's flashlight again. Lifting it, she took in the room's image.

On a sharp inhale, she knew she couldn't wait for backup to arrive. She needed to get outside and help Sully immediately.

"Deacon, come." Cara skirted around the puddles and met the dog on the other side. Wiping her hands on her pants, she reached inside her coat and found her gun, thankful Sully had returned it to its place. She took hold of Deacon's collar and found his leash, and standing, she walked to the front door.

Frigid cold whipped at her face, and she wondered if she was ready for this. Her body still hadn't thawed completely, but she refused to stay inside and do nothing while Sully bled out trying to apprehend this man alone.

I owe him everything.

With that thought in mind, she stepped out into the dark night. The snow had stopped falling at some point, but it left a good foot on the ground.

"Seek Sully," she commanded the dog in a low whisper, putting her hand beneath the dog's nose.

Deacon whined in response, but began tracking.

Quietly, Cara followed the dog until they reached the tree line. Then, the dog turned left while Cara saw two men fighting near the barn on her right. She wondered why Deacon would go in the opposite direction, but that answer would have to wait. Cara pulled on the leash and picked up her pace through the snow.

Beneath her coat, at her back, she removed her handcuffs and had them at the ready to apprehend the man. Mocha had her teeth locked tight around the man's leg, but her grasp wasn't strong enough to deter him. When Cara came within a few feet, she ordered Deacon to hold the man down. The dog launched into the air, sunk his teeth into the man's arm, pulling him down to the ground.

Cara moved in, reaching for his free hand

to pull behind his back. She slapped the first cuff on.

"Release," she commanded. Deacon immediately let go and sat down on his haunches as she took the man's wrist and put the other cuff on it.

Standing, she pulled the man up with her and Sully stood quickly in front of him, reading him his rights.

Cara strained to see through the dark. "Where are you hurt?" she asked Sully.

"It's just a scratch. I'm okay. Let's get him inside and call in the authorities to pick him up."

"I already did. MCK9 is already on the way."

"That could be a while."

"Chase is taking a helicopter. He has Ian also flying in from Montana. But I don't understand how you're standing. You've lost too much blood."

Sully grabbed one arm of the perpetrator while she grabbed the other. They walked toward the house with the dogs beside them. "It's just a scratch. I barely bled."

Cara stepped first into the house and

turned the lights on. She looked down at where Sully had placed her and could see a few bloody spots, now smeared. She led the man toward the kitchen and turned that light on.

"You bled more than you think you did. Look."

Sully inhaled sharply, shaking his head. "Cara, I never came into this room. This is not my blood."

Stunned, Cara looked from Sully to the floor and back. "Well, if it's not yours, then whose is it?"

A strange look came over his face. He tilted his head to the right.

Cara heard the air expelled from her lungs as the realization of what he wasn't saying settled around her. "Jeanette's."

She stepped back until her legs hit a chair. Slowly, she dropped into it. Glancing up at the man in Sully's grasp, she leveled what had to be her most lethal stare she'd ever given anyone. "Where is my sister?"

SEVEN

Sully stood back with Deacon by his side and watched Cara with her team. Chase had arrived with Meadow, Ian, Rocco and Ashley. Being Christmas Eve, they impressed Sully with their dedication to the MCK9 Unit. He didn't know Rocco well, but he knew Ashley, or more like he knew her father. Agent Hanson was a bigwig out at the FBI DC offices. Many believed Ashley was hired on because of her father's influence. Sully would wait on Ashley to prove otherwise before making an assumption of nepotism. So far, she showed seriousness about her job and proved to be dependable. For Cara's sake, he hoped so.

Even though Cara's emotions ran high, and this case was personal, she handled herself with poise and authority. The team had traveled in two helicopters and the choppers had landed in the rear yard. The apprehended perpetrator sat in one, and the pilot prepared to lift off the ground to take him to the closest jail in Jackson. If the man knew where Jennie was, he wasn't saying. Sully didn't believe the man knew anything. Morel sent him to kidnap Cara to use as bait. It's all he would say. He was supposed to bring her in, dead or alive. But he wouldn't say where he was to bring her and to whom.

Sully approached Cara and Chase and told Deacon to sit. Sully then overheard Cara explaining her plan to stay on the ranch. But that was something he couldn't allow.

"That's not possible," he interjected. This was her team, but this was his case. "I need you to return to Elk Valley. I'll take it from here."

Sully expected Cara to fight him, as usual. She didn't like being told what to do, even if it kept her safe. He braced himself for her retort.

"My being here put you in danger. For

that, I am sorry," Cara said, stunning him into silence. She glanced at Chase. "Would you give us a moment, please?"

Chase nodded and stepped away, rejoining a few of his team members with their K-9s.

Once again, Sully braced for what Cara planned to say. He held up his hand to warn her. "Don't fight me on this."

"I won't." She reached for the hand he held up, shaking it. "Thank you."

He stared at where she so formally shook his hand, waiting for her to release him, but she squeezed harder. "For what?" he asked with uncertainty in his voice.

"For coming to my rescue. And for giving Jeanette this life. You did more than I could have ever asked for."

"I'm going to find her, and I'll give her another wonderful life. I promise."

Cara frowned, glancing back at the house. "There's too much blood. I have to face the fact that my sister..." Her throat sounded clogged, and she let go of him to brush at her eyes to wipe away tears.

Sully didn't think he'd ever seen her cry.

Not even the day she said goodbye to her sister forever. And definitely not the day she said goodbye to him. Cara was always stoic, with a tough exterior. But in this moment, the shell of her outward appearance just cracked, and she let him see inside. The rarity of such an occasion touched his heart.

At one time, he would've leaned in and kissed her gently. But those days were long gone. That wouldn't be a line he would ever cross with her again. He knew if he did, then he crossed it alone and with a risk of her putting him back in his place once again.

He kept both his hands at his side but didn't step back. At her height, they matched eye levels, but they were not equals here.

"I'll inform you of every step of the search," Sully said. "I expect to have a team here within the hour." The team wouldn't just be searching for Jennie but a missing marshal as well. One of their own could be in danger, if not already dead, taken out by the cartel to get to Jennie. It wasn't like Logan to fail in his duties.

Cara nodded, already straightening her

shoulders and lifting her chin. The tears were gone. "I would appreciate a brief every two hours." She frowned. "I mean, if that's possible. Sully, I know you don't owe me anything. And you don't work for me."

No, but I care about you.

The words stayed locked inside as he reached for Deacon's collar. "I'll be in touch as often as I can."

Deacon leaned his nose into Sully's hand and immediately alerted. He turned his body toward the front of the ranch, ready to run off, just waiting for the command to seek.

"He's onto something." Sully grabbed the leash and tightened his hold.

Cara followed the dog's attention. "That's the direction we had been going in when we were looking for you." She looked down at her hands, still red with dried blood. "I thought this was your blood, and I had told him to seek you. But…"

"But that's not my blood. That's someone else's. He was tracking whoever's that is, leading you to them."

Cara scanned the terrain behind her, the

direction the K-9 had been taking her in. "Possibly my sister's."

Or my marshal's. "Or one of the gang members themselves." Sully couldn't let her jump to conclusions with speculation. She was too close to this case, but still driven by her profession to catch the bad guys. Could he really send her away now?

The rising sun speckled the new snow like a billion diamonds around them, but the look of determination in Cara's eyes shone brighter than any gem. To deny her this search felt wrong.

"Get Mocha," he said. "We'll check it out. Then you can go."

The look of gratitude filled Cara's face. "Thank you. I know you don't have to let me do this."

In the next second, Cara reached her good arm around his neck and hugged him. The embrace was short and awkward, but it was something she had never done in all the years he had known her. Not even the year they dated. Any act of affection had always been on his part. Cara would never have let herself be so vulnerable.

As she walked to her team to retrieve Mocha, Sully felt sad for her, more than he ever had. That a simple hug was hard for her to offer made him realize the lack of affection she received growing up. Hugging him wasn't easy for her, but she did it. Letting her take the reins in this search wouldn't be easy for him, but he would do it.

Cara returned with Mocha by her side. "I'm ready to check this out. Lead the way."

Sully stepped back and waved her forward. "No. You have the lead."

Cara tilted her head, confusion on her face. "But this is your case. You should call the shots."

"And I say you're in charge now, boss."

Cara frowned. She reached for his chest and tapped him twice. "You were always too good for me, Sully." She turned to her team and began giving orders like the most efficient drill sergeant he had ever heard. Soon they all lined up with their dogs and Cara gave the K-9s the scent they were to track.

As he watched her excel in her FBI duties, Sully feared how finding Jennie's body might change Cara, close her up more. He silently prayed to God to be there for her. Her nightmare, the one thing she tried to stop by putting Jennie into the program in the first place, may be about to come true.

If it was only Deacon tracking, Cara might have thought the dog was bringing them to a dead end. But with her whole MCK9 team's K-9s heading in the same direction, Cara felt confident the trail was hot. Even with a new-fallen snow, the dogs could sniff out her sister's blood and lead the way.

The unit spread out behind in a line about ten feet apart and trudged through the smooth snow that to the human eye appeared tranquil and untouched. But beneath its surface, a trail of blood had been left to follow. Yesterday, before the snow fell, there were footprints that would have shown if her sister walked alone or if someone carried her.

Or dragged her, dead or alive.

Cara refused to let her mind go to that

dark place of the torture Jeanette must have experienced to lose that much blood. It surprised Cara that the interior of the house showed no evidence of foul play. Things appeared to be in their place. Although Cara wouldn't have any idea if that was the case. The life her sister now led was foreign to her, including her home life.

That Sully gave her an artist colony to run stunned Cara with more evidence of his caring heart. She always knew he was a good man, but never to this extent.

That's a lie, and you know it.

Cara's conscience got the better of her. Sully Briggs was the most genuinely caring man she had ever met. And it scared her.

Cara didn't know what to do with such kindness and tenderness. It was foreign to her and made her uncomfortable. She'd much rather go toe to toe with him than hand in hand.

"Mocha is holding her own," Sully said from behind Cara. He had taken her dog and given her Deacon for the lead.

Cara surmised, "She may just be following Deacon's direction. I'm not sure she could handle this on her own. It's still too soon to tell with her."

"You could direct her now to take the lead and find out."

"No. This is too important to risk any misdirection."

"I don't want to sound rude, but every case is important. You'll never know what she's capable of if you don't put her to the test."

Cara looked at the sky and took a deep breath. She knew he was right, but she couldn't let Mocha take the lead. "I just can't, Sully. Right now, I need one hundred percent from everyone. And I need assurance that I'll get it."

"I understand." He walked in silence for a few moments, but she could sense he had more to say, and she probably wouldn't like it.

"Don't hold back on me now," she said. "Say what you need to say."

He chuckled, a deep, rolling, smooth sound that calmed her frayed edges. Still, she braced herself for his painful truth. He always saw too deeply into her. Thankfully, all he saw right now was her back.

"All right, have you ever asked yourself why you must be in control of everyone around you? You know it's impossible, right?"

Daily, she thought. But he didn't have to know that. "Which question do you want me to answer first?"

"Your call."

Cara contemplated her words. She pressed her lips tight and lifted her face to the sun. Its warmth gave her the courage to speak freely. Sully walking behind her helped as well. She wasn't sure if she could be honest to his face.

"Yes, I know it's impossible, but impossible never stopped me. I faced impossible things my whole life and have overcome nearly every single one."

"You've defied the odds—I grant you that. Now for question number one."

Cara smirked and rolled her eyes. "Fine, but let me ask you something first."

"Shoot. My life is an open book."

She nearly stopped and turned around.

"Nothing about you is open. That was our problem. You knew things I could never know."

"I said *my* life was an open book. The lives of the people I protect are not." The seriousness in his voice kept her walking forward, his point made.

Cara questioned how much she wanted to share with him. He knew the crux of her past situation. In a moment of weakness, she had told him her deepest secret fear.

"You know things about me, so I don't think I need to go into them again. But to answer your question about why I need to control my environment, it's because I know what it feels like to have no control. I refuse to be that little girl again. I learned the hard way that no one was coming to help, and I vowed that I would be that help for someone else. *I* would be the cavalry. I don't trust anyone else but myself to fill that role."

"Because no one came for you," he said in a low voice, but it sounded as though he walked closer to her now.

She didn't need to respond. He understood what she was saying.

After another minute of the quiet shushing in the snow, he asked, "What if I told you someone came for you?"

Her foot tripped, and she turned her head slightly. "What are you talking about? No one came for me."

"Jesus did."

Cara chuckled. "I appreciate the thought, but a man from two thousand years ago didn't come to my rescue. I rescued myself."

"Yes, you are a brave, selfless woman. But just consider this for a second. What if God made you this way because He knew you would have to endure a harsh childhood? What if He gave you everything you'd need to rise above your circumstances? What if He's been cheering for you to overcome the things that were meant to destroy you? Would your ideas of Him change, knowing He's been with you the whole time?"

"No. Because I don't need Him to be. In fact, I don't need anyone." Cara could practically hear the frown she knew he was wearing. "Look, if you don't mind, can we change the subject? Because if I let myself believe God has been with me the whole time, then I'd have a hard time trusting anything He says and does."

"Because you'd think He let it happen and didn't care enough," Sully said, speaking her thoughts aloud.

"Seems like a logical conclusion to me."

"God's plans don't always look logical to us. But He promises He will work them out to their proper and perfect end. If we are willing to let go and let Him take over."

Deacon picked up his pace, surprising Cara with a quick pull. Speaking of taking over.

Sully continued, "I think you've dealt with enough bad guys to know they acted of their own free will. Should we punish God for their actions?"

Cara understood what Sully was getting at, but it felt as though he was trying to chip away at her resolve.

A resolve that had taken her years to build up on purpose.

She scanned the area of rolling hills and rugged snowcapped mountains in the distance. The Tetons were a formidable range with a strength she envied. Their gray peaks dominated the horizon, and nothing would ever topple them.

"I'm not punishing God," Cara said. "I just don't want to need Him. I don't want to need anyone."

Deacon stopped abruptly. He pushed through the snow to sniff, turning in a circle until he faced left and started in that direction.

Cara let the dog lead, and Sully stepped beside her. Deacon led them into a thick growth of trees.

"There," Sully said and picked up his steps to pass his dog. Cara struggled to see anything but a forest.

"What do you see?"

Sully knelt and moved the snow-covered brush aside. He revealed a hole in the ground. Cara held her breath as she prepared to find her sister's body. But was that kind of preparation even possible?

She closed in and peered over the opening of the hole but saw no body. Blood was evident but no remains.

"Did an animal take her?"

Sully jumped down, landing with a hard thwack that didn't sound like earth. It sounded like wood.

"A coffin?" Cara asked.

"No. A door." Sully bent and reached for the handle. Before he could lift the cover, a bullet blasted through the wood, sending them both falling backward.

EIGHT

"This is the US Marshals! Stand down!" Sully ordered, with his gun drawn. He kicked open the trapdoor and stood back in case they took another shot at him. "Drop your weapons and put your hands up!"

"Don't shoot! It's me. Jennie!"

He heard the gun fall to the ground and, as he peered inside, he saw Cara's sister with her hands up. "Are you alone?" he asked.

"No. Logan's with me. But he's hurt. Real bad. He's lost a lot of blood. I don't know what to do."

"What is this place?" Sully asked.

"It's a bunker. Logan built it for me in case the ranch was breached. Please help him, Sully!"

Sully had to give a hand to the handler

for his ingenious plan. But first he had to save his life. "We're coming down."

Sully reached a hand up for Cara. His hand hung in the air as he realized she no longer stood above the hole. Moving to the other side, he looked over the edge to see her standing back with the dogs and her team. He locked his gaze on hers and waved her forward.

A small shake of her head told him she would not breach his protocol. She would not alert her sister to her presence. It would be as if she had never been there. True to her word, she only needed to know that her sister was alive and well.

"She'll need a new life anyway," he said. "You were right the whole time. You saved her life."

Cara frowned, not basking in her keen awareness skills, but conflicted. "I don't know if I can say goodbye again. I'm not strong enough."

Sully lifted his hand and chuckled. "You will because you are. Come and meet Jennie. She needs you right now."

Sully wasn't sure if his words broke

through Cara's tough exterior. She gave no expression if they did. Even as she took a step forward and closed the gap between them, he still wasn't sure if she would see Jennie.

At the top of the hole, she said, "Ask Jennie if she wants to see me. I will honor her wishes either way."

Sully didn't like it, but nodded and climbed down into the bunker. It took a moment to adjust his eyes to the small room. Logan had carved a ten-by-ten cavern into the ground, supported with beams and stocked with supplies and a couple of cots. One of which he used on the far side of the bunker. Jennie knelt beside him, speaking softly and encouraging him to wake up.

"Help is on the way. Stay with me, Logan," Jennie pleaded.

The sound of Logan shifting on the cot told Sully that the handler was still alive. "We'll get you out of here, Logan. We have a chopper ready to go."

"I won't leave her," Logan replied in a pained voice. "Morel's men know where she is."

Sully stepped up beside Jennie. "We won't let anything happen to her. We'll take her right to the safe house. You just worry about staying with us." Logan Doyle's blood drenched his clothes. Sully wasn't sure where the injury occurred. "Where were you hit?"

"Near my stomach." A moan escaped his lips. "I don't think it punctured it, though."

"Has the bleeding stopped?"

Jennie looked up at Sully. "I think so. I did the best I could."

He smiled down at her and rubbed her shoulder. He immediately felt the tension coursing through her. "You did good. And well done to you too, Logan, for building this place."

Jennie took Logan's hand, rubbing it with her other hand. "He's so good to me. My only complaint is the peppermint air freshener he hung in here. He didn't know I can't stand the scent. Luis had an addiction to peppermint gum. But other than that, Logan thought of everything."

"You sure gave Morel's men a run for

their money. When they couldn't find you, they got creative."

Jennie asked, "How? What'd they do?"

Sully considered his words. "They went after your sister."

Jennie stood with widened eyes. "Please tell me Cara's okay."

Sully brushed her forearm. "Alive and well. In fact, I'd like to know if you want to see her before you're taken to the safe house."

Jennie quickly looked up at the ceiling. In a breathy whisper, she asked, "Is she here now?"

"Only if you want to see her. If you don't think that'd be a good idea, she will make herself scarce."

Jennie swallowed a few times before tears filled her eyes and she nodded multiple times. "I need to see her. Yes, I want to see my sister."

Sully turned to return to the opening but stopped short.

Cara already stood there, waiting in the shadows. At Jennie's words, Cara stepped forward. In the next second, the sisters ran into each other's arms. He could hear crying from Jennie, but Cara embraced her sister stoically and without emotion.

"Did he hurt you?" Jennie asked through her tears.

"Nothing that won't heal. Don't you worry about me," Cara replied, locking her gaze on Sully. The message was obvious. He could say nothing about her attack. "We don't have much time. We need to get Logan to the hospital and you to the safe house."

Jennie lifted her head and stepped back from her sister. "I have to go to the hospital with him."

Sully said, "Jennie, we can take it from here. Cara will go with you."

Suddenly, Jennie stood just as tall and strong as her sister. She shook her head once. "Where Logan goes, I go."

Sully glanced at Cara. She wore an expression of confusion on her face that must have matched his own.

Cara said to Jennie, "You have an army looking for you. We don't have much time to get you someplace safe. Logan's job as your handler is done. You'll be assigned a new one."

Jennie returned to the edge of the cot, kneeling beside it. She took Logan's hand again and brought it to her lips. "I don't want another handler. I just want Logan."

Sully looked at his agent, realizing what Jennie wasn't saying. Had Logan crossed the line? Relationships were forbidden between the handler and their charge.

"What are you saying?" he asked. "Doyle, explain yourself."

"Sir, nothing has happened. Please, take Jennie and keep her safe."

Jennie reached for Logan's cheek. "I'm not going anywhere without you." She turned back and looked at Sully, a defiant lift to her chin. "I love him. And he loves me. I would rather die than be apart from him."

Sully glanced at Cara, and he thought he saw flames in her eyes. He lifted his hand to hold her back, but he wasn't fast enough.

Cara's drill sergeant's voice was back. "After everything I have given up for you, after everything I have done to keep you safe, you would choose to throw it all away? You *will* go to that safe house, even if I have to drag you there myself. And that's an order, Jeanette."

Sully knew he should jump in and take over, but Cara's statement about all she gave up startled him. What did she mean?

He told himself that it was about giving up her only family. But what if that included him? Had Cara cared more about him than he had thought?

"The road is open, and the truck is running," Chase informed Cara back at the ranch. "We'll still fly Logan to the hospital, but the rest of the team will need to drive back. Sully's SUV is drivable. I just need to know what to do with Jennie. She's adamant about going with Logan, but Sully says she must go with him."

"Sully's right. She'll be going back into witness protection and will go to the safe house right away. Every moment that she's out, her life is at risk."

Chase nodded but didn't move to follow

the orders. He hesitated a little too long for Cara's comfort.

"Is there a problem, Rawlston?" she asked with a tilt of her head. Ordinarily, she wouldn't invite an opinion, but she had known Chase long before their time together in DC. Their careers intersected many times when she lived and worked in Wyoming. She might have even considered him a friend if she wasn't his boss.

"That depends on who you ask. I completely understand the necessity of getting Jennie to the safe house. But, ma'am, there are enough of us to keep watch. It seems almost cruel to separate her from Logan when she..."

"She what? Loves him? All the more reason to make a clean break quickly. She'll love again. Don't worry, Chase. This is how my sister is. When she's in her next life, she'll fall for the next handsome man that smiles at her. This is why she's in this mess with Luis to begin with. The team has put their lives at risk for her. The least she can do is follow orders, so no one gets hurt."

Chase frowned. "All I know is that giving up someone you love can fill a person's life with no hope."

Cara sighed and walked to the table, taking the chair at the head of the long oak. "But you found someone. You're about to be remarried. Zoe is a wonderful mother. You're going to be a father again. There *is* hope in loving again. You've just proved it."

Chase nodded and stepped up to the adjacent chair, placing his hands on the top rung. "But it took years. And there's no guarantee that Jennie will. Look, all I'm asking for is if she can go with him to the hospital to make sure that he makes it? At least give her that peace."

Cara looked up at her team leader and remembered the pain he felt for years after losing his wife and daughter in that bomb.

"Peace," she said. "Peace comes from order."

"I used to believe that too. But now, I know that true peace is not something we can create ourselves. It comes by letting go and letting God bless us. It's committing our work to Him and letting Him establish our plans. He's in control."

Cara did her best not to roll her eyes as she mumbled, "You sound like Sully."

Chase smirked. "So you've heard this before."

"It's not that I have anything against God—it's that I've learned I need to make my peace. My sister will do the same. It will just take time. She'll find a new life and make her own peace."

"Tell that to Ian," Chase said, referencing their team member Ian Carpenter, who had spent time in WITSEC, the witness protection program, with a new identity. "It's not always about making a new life. It's about getting your old life back. Jennie's done well in her new life. She knows more than any of us what it's like to start over and knows what it'll take to do it again."

Cara folded her arms on the table and eyed her team leader suspiciously. "Are you suggesting that she not return to the program?"

Chase put his hands in the air and shook his head. "Not at all. If that's what keeps her alive, then that's her only option. I'm just saying ten years have gone by for her.

She's not in the same place she was when she went in. The clock didn't stop for her, even though your image of her may have stopped for you. She's a different person now, and I'm not talking about her new identity. A lot has happened in this time frame. I believe she's fallen in love and now has more to lose. Let her go to the hospital. I'll put both Ashley and Ian on as her detail. Along with their K-9s, no one will get through. She'll be safe. If she has to say goodbye to Logan, give her some time to do it."

Cara dropped her forehead in her hand as she contemplated all that could go wrong. Morel had his soldiers all over the world, most of them well trained in prisons. They held no code of honor and wouldn't think twice of taking out the team to get to Jennie.

"You're asking a lot of me. I'm responsible if someone gets hurt, or worse."

"I understand, boss. But it's Christmas Eve."

Cara took a moment and realized he was right. After such a harrowing few, she'd lost track of days—not that she had any big plans for the holiday. She frowned at the thought.

"I suppose it'd be nice to spend Christmas Eve with my sister one last time."

He smiled. "There's that too. I'll make sure you're not disturbed, and you have this time together."

Standing, she reached for Chase's hand to shake. But just before she made contact, the kitchen door opened, and Sully stood in the doorway. His face was pale, and his chest heaved as though he'd run the whole way. Something was wrong.

Cara dropped her hand and walked his way. "Logan? I thought they stabilized him."

Sully shook his head and reached a hand to her. Cara closed the gap and took it, never losing eye contact. "Your sister..." He shook his head and closed his eyes.

"What about her? Morel?"

"Not yet. But I'd say anytime now. She stole my car."

"What?" Cara dropped his hand and tried to move past him to the door.

"They're gone. I thought they were in the helicopter. When I went to check on them, it was empty, and the SUV was missing."

"She took the SUV? What is she thinking?"

"There's more," Sully said. "I was just radioed in the chopper that Luis Morel was released early because of the holiday."

Cara took a few seconds to process this information. Slowly, she turned and locked gazes with Chase. "Now, I'm *really* not feeling too peaceful about this situation. Get the helicopter ready. We fly in ten minutes."

NINE

As the pilot flew them over the towering treetops, Sully scanned the roads below, looking for his vehicle. Cara sat beside him, looking out the other side, and they each wore a set of headphones. Although, she had yet to say a word since the helicopter lifted off from the ranch. Up front, Chase sat beside the pilot. He had left his K-9 with the team, but Deacon and Mocha were secure in their crates in the chopper's rear. Sully thought it best to bring their dogs, just in case they ran into trouble.

"Even if Morel was released this morning, it would take him a few hours to get here from California," Sully spoke his thoughts aloud.

Cara stayed facing toward the window. "If that's supposed to comfort me, it's not."

She leaned closer to the window but shook her head. "The tops of these cars all look the same. If only we knew a direction that she went in. She knows this area better than either of us. She could be anywhere from here to Yellowstone. Or maybe she went south into Colorado."

Sully replied, "Logan needs medical attention. If she loves him as she says she does, that would be her only concern."

"Chase," Cara said through the microphone. "Find the nearest hospitals. Have the team call to see if Jennie brought Logan into any of them. Tell them to be on the lookout for her and to notify us the moment she walks in."

"You got it," Chase said, picking up his phone.

Cara rubbed her forehead, removing her glasses to touch her eyes. A quiet sniff captured Sully's attention.

Cara was crying?

"We're going to find her and get her to safety," he assured her.

She put her glasses back on and looked

out the window. Shaking her head, she said, "Was it all for nothing?"

"Was what for nothing?"

"Everything." Cara faced him. "All you did for her. Aren't you the least bit angry about her throwing it all away?"

Sully thought about the question, but not for long. The answer was simple. "Not at all. I did the best job I could. Whatever happens after is out of my control. I'm not responsible for the outcome. That will now be between Jennie and God. But, Cara, you should know, everything I did for Jennie wasn't for her. It was for you."

"Me?"

"You asked me to give her a good life, one she could love. It was all for you."

Cara bent her head and broke eye contact with him. "You were always so good to me. I don't—"

"Don't say it," he said, covering her hand on her lap. "Just say thank you. I mean, if you want to."

"Thank you, Sully. But it should be Jennie telling you that. And she should be right here to do it." Cara turned her palm up and grasped his fingers. "I don't owe you a thank-you. I owe you an apology."

"For what?"

She sent him a sideways glance. "Uh… for walking out on you, of course."

Sully chuckled uncomfortably. He caught Chase removing his headset and knew the man was giving them privacy.

Sully let go of Cara's hand, feeling unsure about hearing what she was about to say. "Leave it be. There's no reason to rehash those days. You were right—we never would have made it anyway. Don't let today's events cloud the truth."

Cara nodded and faced the window again. "I suppose you're right." She glanced back at him with the slightest frown. "But I guess we'll never know, will we?"

Twice in one day, Sully questioned Cara's words. First back in the bunker when she mentioned how much she had given up, and now this reference to never finding out if they could have survived as a couple.

Sully faced forward, not letting himself dig into her words. He caught Chase putting the headphones back on.

"Boss?" Chase said. "No hospital has seen Jennie or Logan come in. Any ideas?"

Cara glanced Sully's way with a question in her eyes. "You know this area. Would there be any other places she might bring him?"

Sully shrugged. "Hospitals, or maybe a nearby clinic, would have been my guess."

"Did you try the clinics, Chase?" Cara asked quickly.

"Not yet. I'm on it." Chase removed his headset again and typed on his phone.

Cara fisted her hands in her lap and closed her eyes. She looked like she was at her wit's end. She looked like she was losing control.

But control was a facade, and it always had been. How to get her to understand this was beyond him.

Sully closed his eyes and prayed for God's guidance and words that would break through the tough exterior of Cara's beliefs. He knew those beliefs were planted in the pain of her childhood, and it would take the power of God to pull those roots up. Sully hadn't been enough to help her ten years ago, and he wouldn't be now.

"I'm sure this isn't how you planned to spend Christmas Eve," Sully said.

Cara shook her head. "No, but it's part of the job. I'm sure the entire team would much rather be hanging boughs of holly than tracking down my foolish sister. But they won't complain, and neither will I."

"What had you planned to do?"

Cara stared out the window. "I was invited to a friend's house for dinner. Now that I think of it, I don't think I told them I wasn't coming." She reached into her coat pocket and removed her phone to type out a text. "There," she said and hit Send. "I hope they aren't too mad."

"Mad about what? You just said this is part of the job. They must know that things come up for you. Bad guys don't follow a calendar."

"No, but I made a commitment. I said I would be there."

"This is out of your control."

Cara smirked his way and narrowed her gaze. "Don't remind me."

"It's really hard for you to let things go, isn't it?"

She shrugged. "It's dangerous to let things go. People get hurt when I do."

"You let *me* go." Sully said the words before he thought them through. He was about to apologize, but she spoke first.

"Yeah, and it hurt."

Sully paused. Once again, Cara struck him speechless with her words. But even though her words led him to believe Cara had suffered from their breakup, her aloof composure said otherwise. She acted as though it wasn't a big deal.

He looked down at his hands and said what was on his mind. "But not enough to come back."

He knew he sounded flippant and maybe a little whiny, but it felt good to talk freely with the big boss of the MCK9 and FBI Special Agent in Charge. He always knew she would eventually outrank him in their pursuits, but it never bothered him until she turned her back on him and all they had. Then he felt inconsequential.

He felt forgotten.

He felt small.

"You should be happy I didn't," she said. "You would hate me by now."

Hate you? I loved you.

"Why do you say that?" Sully asked instead.

"Sully, I'm not partner material. The truth is, I would never have been able to rely on you. I don't trust anyone but myself. It's why I left a hospital bed and hopped a plane to fly out to Wyoming."

"The whole 'it's not you, it's me' excuse? You can't be serious," Sully said pointedly. "You never let me prove to you that you could rely on me."

"Exactly. That would mean…"

"Letting go," he finished for her. "It would mean choosing to believe in us. Tell me, did I let you down when you asked me to find a wonderful home for your sister?"

Cara frowned and looked out the window. Eventually, she shook her head. Without turning back to him, she whispered, "When I saw what you did for her, I knew you went above and beyond what I asked for. You didn't just give her a home. You granted her dreams."

"I wanted to give you yours as well. What's your dream, Cara? What do you wish for more than anything else?"

"You're being frivolous and ridiculous," she said, but didn't turn his way. "I don't need anything. I'm perfectly content where I am."

"I don't believe you. Deep down inside you, there's a little girl who once had a dream that was squashed. You say that you can only rely on yourself, but you've let that little girl down. What did she dream of? What was that little girl's dream? Be honest."

Slowly, Cara turned his way. Sully saw Chase fit his headphones back on. He wanted to tell the man to hold off sharing his update. He may never get Cara to be so open with him again.

"The team found her," Chase said, turning his head to look at Sully. "Or at least they found your car. And you were right. She took Logan to a clinic. Beacon Falls

Medical Clinic outside Jackson. We haven't gone in yet. What do you want them to do?"

Sully caught Cara watching him intently. Whose call would it be? She said she couldn't rely on him, and he knew his next move would prove if she was right about him or not. He also knew he had to make this call, not her. Legally, Jennie was his responsibility.

"How far are we from the clinic?" he asked.

Chase looked at the pilot to ask.

The pilot held his hand up with all five fingers. "Five minutes," he shouted.

Cara tilted her head. "A lot can happen in five minutes."

She was right. If they scared Jennie, she could run again. If Luis's men were already on her, she could be dead by then.

Sully took a deep breath and decided. Looking directly at Cara, he said, "Send them in."

Cara's eyes widened as she pursed her lips. Apparently, he had chosen wrong.

"You would rather the team wait?" he asked. "Or did you want to be the one to go in? They're your team, Cara. How much do you trust them?"

Chase looked behind the front seat at Cara. "They're the best, boss. I have complete faith in them to handle this correctly. I know this is your sister and personal to you, but you can count on them."

Cara closed her eyes for a moment before nodding. "They're a good team and have proved themselves this year with the Rocky Mountain Killer. Still, please tell them to be careful. Luis Morel is a career criminal the likes they have never seen."

Chase turned back with a nod and set out to warn the MCK9 team. When Sully looked at Cara, he found her slightly smiling at him. If all went down poorly, he would still be to blame.

"You trusted me with your sister before," he said. "You can trust me again. You can trust me always."

Cara faced forward without responding. The next five minutes ticked on in excruciating slowness. When the clinic roof came into view, he spotted his SUV as well as a few others from the team. There were a few cars he didn't recognize, most likely the employees of the clinic. Off in the distance, he could also see the red-and-blue flashing lights of the local police racing toward the clinic. Then he saw an ambulance speeding behind the police cars.

"What's going on, Chase?" Sully asked.

Chase held up his finger for a moment as he read his texts. "She's not there. But Logan is. He's unconscious. There's also a doctor and nurse who are dead."

Cara dropped her head and clasped her hands in her lap. "We're too late. Morel has her."

Sully had to agree but kept his comments to himself. After a moment, he thought he saw Cara's shoulders trembling. In the next second, clear liquid fell on her hands, and he realized she was crying.

Sully reached a hand to her, but Cara quickly pushed him away and turned to face the window.

"Whether you want to believe it, I'm on your side. I always have been. You may think you survived on your own, but the truth is you survived because there are people rooting for you and praying for you, and I am one of them. I'm not your enemy."

"No."

Sully frowned, frustrated in her ability to believe him. Then she turned his way and let him see the tears streaming down her face.

"You're not my enemy. You're my dream. But, Sully, dreams are for free spirits like my sister. Dreams are for people who chase sunsets. I chase bad guys before they can hurt anyone else. I don't dare dream. Dreaming is a waste of time for me. So don't bother praying for me anymore. Just be real with me. That's all I want."

TEN

As soon as the helicopter landed in the rear yard of the medical clinic, Cara opened her door and jumped down to the ground. Before she made it to the back entrance, Sully ran beside her with Mocha and Deacon. Thankfully, the man let her confession go…for now. She knew him well enough to know he wouldn't let it go forever. It had been foolish and risky of her to admit such things. It had been…well…it had been a loss of control.

Never again.

Cara held her arm up to stop Sully from entering the building. "Wait until I hear if the scene is under control. Chase, what's the situation with the team?"

Chase headed up to her side. "We're clear to enter. Logan just came to, and the paramedics are prepping him for transport. The scene is secure, and they already know we're here."

Cara nodded but still shouted, "FBI!" to announce herself as she stepped inside.

The MCK9 team was already processing the scene and covered the two bodies. Bullet holes riddled the walls and Cara figured Morel's man must have come in with guns blazing. At least two people were killed, but what about Jennie?

Cara stepped up to the stretcher with Logan on it. His eyes were closed. "Is he coherent?" she asked the paramedic.

Logan turned his head slightly her way. His voice was weak. "Find her. Please."

"Was she shot?"

He shook his head back and forth. "I failed her." His voice caught and sounded gargled with tears that dripped down the sides of his head.

"I need you to stay with me. Did you see who took her? Were they in a car?"

He shook his head again. "I didn't hear a vehicle. I couldn't do anything to stop him. I didn't get a good look. One moment, the doctor stood beside me, and the next…he fell onto me, pulling me down with him. I could hear Jennie screaming, but I lost consciousness once I hit the floor."

Cara sought Chase. He stood by the exit with Sully and the dogs. "Start a search through the woods out back."

Deacon sat in perfect compliance, but Mocha had her nose to the floor, sniffing. Cara frowned, about to give up on the dog. Mocha just couldn't follow commands.

"Leave Mocha behind. She'll hold you up," Cara said, moving to take the dog's leash from Sully.

"Wait," Sully said, kneeling. "She found something."

Cara narrowed her gaze on a tiny piece of paper. She reached for a pair of latex gloves on the table and picked up the tiny square. On the other side of the paper was the label for a stick of peppermint gum.

"Peppermint gum," Cara said, wondering if it was important at all, or if it had been here before Morel's man arrived. There was no way to tell.

"Did you say peppermint?" Logan asked from the stretcher.

Cara stepped up beside him again. "Yeah, why? Does it have any importance?"

"Luis used to chew peppermint gum all the time. Jennie can't stand the smell."

Sully said, "Right, she said that at the bunker about you putting a peppermint air freshener in there. It was her only complaint."

Cara looked down at the piece of paper and considered what this evidence meant. "But if the shooter left this here, then it wasn't one of Morel's men at all."

Sully shook his head. "It was Luis Morel himself."

Even though Cara had figured this was the case, hearing Sully say the words felt like a punch to her gut.

"Luis took her? She'll be dead within the hour." Logan tried to sit up.

Cara put her arm on his chest to push him back down. "You're not going anywhere."

"I have to. She was my charge. I have to find her."

"You're going to the hospital. *We're* going

to find her." Cara nodded to the paramedics to take him. She held the wrapper beneath Mocha's nose. "Seek."

Immediately, the K-9 put her nose to the floor and turned for the rear entrance. The hunt was on.

Cara passed the wrapper to each member of the team for their dogs, and soon the MCK9 group was heading into the woods, following Luis's favorite scent.

Sully stepped up beside her. "Mocha came through."

Cara had to agree, though she still wasn't sure about the dog's future. "It's promising, but I'm not ready to rely on her completely. She could have just been curious."

"Or she wants to earn your trust."

Before Cara could respond, she heard a helicopter firing up. It had to be Morel's getaway. Cara picked up her pace to an all-out run. "Up ahead! Quick, before they fly out!"

Sully ran up beside her, keeping her pace. She pushed herself harder, and when she broke through the trees, the helicopter tilted as it lifted off the ground.

"Stop!" she shouted at the top of her lungs, pulling her gun. But before she could hold it out, bullets sprayed in her direction from the helicopter.

"Get down!" Sully shouted beside her, pulling her back behind a rock. They riddled the place she had been standing with bullets. "He'll kill you first. You're her only family. Let us handle this."

"He's getting away!" Cara never felt so useless. She knew Sully was right, but how could she just stand down? How could she let Luis get away? How could she let go and let everyone else handle this? What if they failed?

She would fail. After everything she did to protect her sister, it all would be for nothing. All her plans and sacrifices were for nothing.

Her plans, not God's.

Cara sought the words Sully had told her about how the Lord would establish her plans. And how He would work it all out to its proper end.

But that meant letting go and no longer

being in control of the situation. *Was I ever really in control to begin with?*

Cara knew the answer, but it didn't make stepping back any easier. Taking a deep breath, she watched the helicopter rise to about ten feet in the air, then looked at Sully and nodded for him to take over.

In the next second, Sully turned back to the team, shouting orders to each of them. He sent Chase and Ashley to his far right. Meadow and Ian went to the left. Rocco was told to handle the opposite side. Suddenly, Cara's team had surrounded the helicopter and opened fire. From her vantage point, she could see Ashley stand behind a tree. She held her gun close to her chest and stepped out. But Cara noticed the officer didn't unload her weapon, but narrowed her focus on something in particular. Suddenly, she took five shots, and in the next second, the helicopter spun around in circles.

Cara realized Ashley had targeted the helicopter's tail, rendering it useless. The helicopter spun itself right into the ground, its blades still swirling until one hit a rock, coming to a grinding stop. If there was still any doubt in Ashley's abilities as an agent, she'd just put them to rest. So what if her father was an FBI head honcho? Ashley continued to earn her place on the team all on her own.

Sully jumped to his feet and waved everyone in from all sides. "Go, go, go, go!" he shouted, and the MCK9 team jumped into action in perfect unison.

Cara crouched low and watched the handlers with their K-9s take down Luis Morel and two of his men on the helicopter. She had never been so proud of this team as she was in this moment. Seeing the threat vanquished, she sought her sister.

Jeanette appeared to be slouched in a rear chair. Suddenly, Cara realized her sister may already be dead. She nearly jumped to her feet and ran into the fray. This morning, she probably would have. Instead, she looked at Sully and waited for his orders.

As if reading her mind, he turned to her and gave her the nod to go.

Cara raced from behind the rock and across the clearing. The helicopter had landed on a tilt, and she had to pull herself up inside. She immediately saw her sister had a gash on the side of her head and she was unconscious. Cara felt her neck for a pulse and thanked God when she felt the beats of life still in her sister.

"Jeanette, it's me, Cara. You're safe now. Wake up." Cara tapped her sister's cheek a few times, but Jeanette only moaned.

The helicopter tilted as Sully climbed up. "Here, let me try this." He cracked open a tiny vial and put it under Jeanette's nose.

"Where'd you get that?" Cara asked.

"Smelling salts. I grabbed them off the wall in the clinic before we headed out."

"Brilliant," Cara said. "Why didn't I think of that?"

Sully chuckled as he waved the vial closer to Jeanette's nose. "That's why we make a good team, boss."

Before Cara could process his words, Jeanette jolted awake and immediately screamed in fright. Cara could only focus on calming her sister down and holding her tight.

"We've apprehended Luis. He's going

back to jail for a very long time. I'll make sure of it."

Jeanette continued to fight and flail against Cara. She burst out in tears.

Sully put his hand on Jeanette's head, pulling her attention up to him. "You're safe again, Jennie. And so is Logan. He's at the hospital now. He's going to be okay. You're safe. Do you understand what I'm saying?"

Jeanette let out a deep sigh and focused on Sully. Slowly, she nodded and looked down at Cara. A smile flickered on her parched lips. She touched her hand to Cara's cheek. "My sister."

Cara stood and brought Jeanette to her shaky feet. Wrapping an arm around her, Cara led her out of the helicopter and steered her away from where Luis was in handcuffs and being taken to a police car.

Jeanette leaned on Cara's shoulder, reminding her of the years she protected her little sister from their father.

But she wasn't a little girl anymore. And it was time to grow up.

"You put many people in danger today," Cara said. "Why would you leave like that?"

"I know. I'm sorry. I just wasn't ready to say goodbye yet. I just wanted a little more time with him."

Cara pursed her lips, stopping herself from saying her sister's answer was frivolous and irresponsible. Her decision to walk away from Sully ten years ago had been quick, like tearing off a Band-Aid, but how many times had she wished for one more hour together?

"You really love him?" Cara asked.

Jeanette nodded her head to let out a little cry. "It's going to be so hard not to have him in my life anymore." She turned to look Cara in the eye. "How did you do it? When I heard you left Sully, I didn't believe it. I felt so guilty. I knew you did it because of me."

"I did what had to be done. And so will you."

They walked the rest of the way to the helicopter and boarded in the back. Sully returned the dogs to their crates and sat up front. The pilot climbed into the cockpit and looked back at them.

"Where to?"

Both Jeanette and Sully looked at Cara, waiting for her to decide. Would it be the safe house, or would it be a hospital to say goodbye to Logan?

Cara sought Sully's expectant face. She knew he would go along with whatever she decided, but maybe her plans weren't the right ones right now.

"I suppose a stop at the hospital would be okay. Morel's in custody." She looked at Jeanette. "We'll give you fifteen minutes to say goodbye."

Jeanette inhaled a shaky breath but nodded. "Thank you. I know I don't deserve that."

Cara faced forward and caught Sully smiling at her. He gave her a quick wink and turned back around to face forward in the front. She bit back a smile and pressed her lips tight, finding a tree outside to focus on. Slowly, a thought came to her. She would also need to say goodbye to him. Somehow, the idea of walking away again seemed impossible. It made no sense, as the two of them had parted ways so long ago, disconnecting their lives from each other, other than the occasional forced work proximity.

But she would do it because it was the right thing to do. Her sister would be back under his charge and put into witness protection once again. He would give her another good life, and Cara fully believed he would. The way he came through with the MCK9 team back at the clearing, she knew he would come through with her sister as well.

The flight to the hospital was quick and quiet, with no one speaking. It was as though they all could feel the rising tension of what these last fifteen minutes would be for each of them. The helicopter landed on top of the building, and even their walk through the hospital to Logan's room mounted with more dread.

They entered the room to find him sitting up in the bed with his eyes closed. Jeanette approached his side slowly.

"Logan? Are you awake?"

Immediately, his eyelids flew open, and he reached for her. "I've been sitting here praying for you. Oh, thank God you're okay." He brought her hands to his lips and kissed them repeatedly.

"And you're okay too?" Jeanette asked.

He nodded. "I just came out of surgery. I'm all stitched up. I'm going to be fine."

Tears streamed down Jeanette's cheeks. "Logan, I can't stay. I have to go back into the program."

Logan smiled big. "I know. You're going to have a good life. Sully will make sure, right, Sully? Please give her a good life."

Sully said, "The best." He looked at Cara. "Shall we give them a few minutes alone?"

Cara couldn't see why not. "We'll be right outside. Fifteen minutes."

Cara and Sully turned to the door, but when they reached it, Logan called out to Sully.

"I quit," he said, halting their steps. Turning back, Logan held Jeanette's hands in his. He looked at her. "I love you. I have always loved you. Wherever you go, I want to be with you. Whatever identity and home you're given will be mine as well. I mean, if you'll have me."

Jeanette brushed his hair from his eyes. "Have you? But that would mean you give up your whole life and your family."

"You'll be my family." He looked at Sully. "Do you accept my resignation?"

"Have you thought this through?" Sully asked. "This is not something to enter lightly. You'll be sacrificing a lot."

"I'm a handler in WITSEC. I know what it means. And yes, I have thought it through, and I've prayed about it. I know this is where God is leading me. I know Jennie is my future."

Sully nodded and glanced Cara's way. As she watched her sister lean in to kiss Logan, Cara tried to be happy for her. And she was, but there was still a part of her that wondered if her sister realized how many people gave up so much for her happiness.

"I'll wait in the hall," Cara said and turned away from the joyful couple. She could hear Sully explaining to the two of them what would happen next for them. They would be given new names as a married couple. Cara continued to walk down the hall until their voices became muffled. She didn't want to know the details, nor could she. As she reached the elevator, her phone rang.

She retrieved the phone from her pocket, needing to jump back into her work. As long as she was busy chasing bad guys, she didn't feel any pain. It was how she got through the last ten years, and it would be how she got through the rest of life.

Chase's number showed on the screen. "What's up?" Cara asked.

"Morel made a break for it when he reached the police department. There appears to be some sort of breach in the force. One of his soldiers must've infiltrated. Where are you?"

Cara swung back around to look at Logan's door at the end of the hall. She was the only person in the wing. She took a few steps, slowly at first, then speeding up.

"We're at the hospital. We'll fly out to the safe house right away." She hung up the phone and raced into the room. "No time to pack. We need to get to the roof. Now."

"But he can't walk," Jeanette whined. "He just had surgery."

Cara pulled up a wheelchair from against the wall. "Sully. Help him into it."

"What's happened?" Sully asked as he followed her orders.

"Morel's on the loose. Made a break for it at the police station. We need to get to the roof and fly to the safe house."

Sully growled under his breath as he wheeled Logan to the door. "I should have planned for something like this."

"No one could have planned for something like this," Cara said. "Not even me. The man was in custody. We had him."

"Then the police took him into custody. You said yourself he has soldiers all over this world. Sadly, some of those soldiers wear police uniforms."

They took the elevator to the roof and rushed out the metal door to the helicopter. Cara ran ahead of them to open the helicopter door, hearing the dogs barking profusely in their crates. Then she saw the pilot slumped dead over the controls, a bullet hole in his forehead.

Cara circled, eyeing every hidden location on the rooftop. She drew her gun. "Get back!" she shouted to everyone. "Get back inside!"

"Not without you," Sully said, drawing his own weapon.

"Get my sister to safety!"

Sully ran back to the metal roof door just as a bullet pinged off it. Jeanette pushed Logan through the door, but Sully continued to hold the door open.

"Hurry!" he shouted. "Cara!"

In the same moment, Cara spotted the shooter from behind a mechanical box. The man, dressed in all black, pointed his weapon at Sully.

"No!" Cara struggled to give her orders, feeling her throat close. She ran toward the man. "Drop your weapon!"

But the man took his shot, then turned the gun on her.

Cara glanced at Sully to see he'd dodged the bullet. He held his own gun, pointed in her direction.

No, not at her. He pointed his weapon at the man behind her.

Sully shot off multiple bullets as pain ripped through her back, sending her flying and landing facedown on the concrete.

A bullet struck her, and the world around her fell silent.

ELEVEN

Sully dropped to his knees, scrambling to Cara while still shooting at one of Morel's men. Three more shots landed in the shooter's chest, taking him out completely. Scanning the rooftop for any other shooters, Sully reached Cara and scooped an arm under her to pull her toward the door.

She groaned but opened her eyes to look at him. She reached her hand to his cheek. "We should have gone to the safe house. This is my fault."

Sully shook his head. "No. I would've made the same call. Hang in there. I'm going to get you downstairs. The doctors will fix you right up good as new."

Her eyes closed, but she opened them wide. "Sully, I'm so sorry. I wish… I know I hurt you. I wish I was stronger than I am."

He cradled her close and lifted her. "What are you talking about? You're the strongest woman I know. In fact, I'm pretty sure you'd top a few men I know too."

At the door, she said, "Listen to me. There may not be time."

Sully's ears blared in defiance at her words. He refused to listen to them. Opening the door, he saw Jennie and Logan were gone. He could only hope Logan was smart enough to hide Jennie someplace safe. Sully couldn't protect Jennie while getting Cara into the ER.

"Listen to me. That's an order, Sully." Her threat sounded strained and fell short of her typical position.

"No, you listen to me. You're going to be fine." He raced down the stairs three floors, doing his best not to jostle her.

"I never wanted to leave you," she said. Her eyes drifted closed and flew open again. "I did what had to be done, but I didn't want to. I wanted a life with you. You made me..." She swallowed hard. "You made me feel safe."

Her statement proved to be a lie. As he

held her, feeling her blood seep out on his hands, he hadn't been able to keep her safe at all.

"You made the right choice, love. Don't think twice about it. I would have held you back. You were meant for so much more. I'm so proud of you. I don't think I ever told you that." He leaned down and kissed her forehead in sheer desperateness. "So proud of you."

Cara's face paled quickly before him, and her eyelids continued to flicker. At the ground floor, Sully burst through the door to the ER.

"I need a doctor!" he shouted as he reached the desk.

A nurse stood and came around the front. "What happened?" she asked as she pulled up a gurney.

"Gunshot in the back. Shooter on the roof."

"What?"

"I'll tell you after. Just get her into surgery. Go!"

The nurse pushed the bed down the hall, but Sully saw Cara's hand reach out to him.

"Sully!" she cried out.

He moved to keep up with her. "I forgive you. Don't worry. Just fight, Cara. Please, fight!"

"Don't leave me, Sully!"

His shoes squeaked on the sterile white floor as he came to an abrupt halt.

Cara reached the doors that he couldn't bypass, but it was her words that stopped him cold.

In a whisper, he said, "Oh, Cara, I never have."

Watching her go, he felt as useless as before, standing alone as the doors swung shut.

But he didn't have to be useless.

He would find Jennie and get her to the safe house. He could do that for Cara while she fought for her life. *God, help her fight. Please, give her Your strength so she can live. She still has so much to do. This world needs her. Mocha needs her.*

Jennie needs her.

Sully stopped short of admitting that he needed her and jumped into action. Raising his voice as he turned and ran for the security booth at the front of the emergency room, he shouted, "Lock this place down! No one in and no one out. We have one active shooter extinguished on the roof, but there could be more."

The security guard tried to ask a question, but Sully showed his badge and kept giving orders to secure the building and call the police. The guard picked up the phone and made the calls throughout the hospital. Doors closed automatically while sirens rang off, with red flashing lights down the halls.

Sully ran for the stairwell again, making it to the roof in record time. It wasn't until he ran out into the sunlight that he realized his hands and clothes were covered in Cara's blood.

Too much blood.

He pushed the thought aside, believing she would make it. She had to. And he had to find Jennie and Logan.

Running for the helicopter, Sully kept his gun in front of him. He opened the rear door and freed Deacon from his crate.

"Guard," Sully ordered while he unlatched

Mocha's crate. The dog whined and shied away. Maybe Cara was right about the dog. It might be best to leave her behind. "Cara needs you, Mocha. Now's the time to show you're up for the task. Come."

Sully stepped back and took up Deacon's leash. He gave Mocha a few seconds to decide. If she refused, he would have his answer about her ability to be a K-9 officer.

She didn't move.

Sully reached to close the door, but Mocha let out a loud bark and bolted from her crate and out of the helicopter door. She ran past Sully and leaped into the air. Sully turned just in time to see Mocha take down another gunman.

The man cried out in pain from Mocha's teeth, holding him in a tight grip. Sully ran to the man and handcuffed him.

"Release," Sully ordered, commanding Mocha to stand down. To the man, he demanded, "Where's Morel?" Sully pulled the man to his feet.

The man turned his head and spit at him, but Sully pushed the man forward to walk. "That's how you want to play it? Just remember, you mean nothing to Luis Morel. This is your last offer to play nice. Tell me where he is."

"You'll never find him. He'll find you, and by then you're a dead man." The man laughed. "Just like your FBI girlfriend."

Sully felt his lip curl at the back of the man's head. He bit his tongue from saying what was really on his mind. "I will find him. You can count on it."

Sully brought Morel's soldier down the stairs of the hospital. On the ground floor, police swarmed about. He approached two in uniform. "Can you hold on to this one?" He knew his comment came across a bit too snidely, but so be it.

The two officers nodded. "I guess we have that coming," one of them said. "Rest assured, we have dealt swiftly with our weakest link. It won't happen again."

"Great to hear. I'm going to need a few vests. I need to get two people out of this hospital safely. I'll also need a car by the entrance."

The two men found the items Sully needed and then led the man out the doors into the back of the cruiser. Satisfied, Sully returned to his task of finding Jennie. This time, he didn't have anything of hers to give to the dogs.

But he had something of Logan's.

With his free hand, Sully reached into his pants pocket and removed the badge Logan had given him after the US Marshal had given him his notice. He stared at the badge and thought of Logan's choice to give up his life for the woman he loved. Sully thought back ten years to the time Cara walked out of his life because of the conflict of interest between them. He never once thought about quitting his job and wondered if that's what she had wanted of him. But if he had done that, he would have had no say in where her sister lived, and he would have never found her this week when her life was being threatened. As much as it hurt to watch Cara leave him, he knew it was for the best for Jennie's sake. He fully believed Cara would say the same thing. Her sister's safety always came first.

Sully returned to where he last saw Jennie and Logan and was glad to see Mocha take the lead in the search.

"You'll make a great K-9," he said. Sully could only hope that Cara would make it through to see the dog earn her badge. He prayed this would be the case as the dogs tracked Logan's scent. Within fifteen minutes, the path ended at a door.

"Logan? It's Sully. It's safe to come out."

No response followed.

Just because the path ended at this door didn't mean the two of them entered this room alive. They could have very well been killed and dropped behind this door.

Sully gave the command to the dogs to be on full alert. He readied his gun and turned the knob. With a quick turn, he pulled the door wide and maneuvered his body out of view.

A quick gasp came from inside, telling him at least one person was alive.

"Jennie, it's me. Sully. It's safe to come out. I need to get you to the safe house immediately."

"And Logan?"

"Yes. And Logan. We need to move fast."

In the next second, Jennie stepped into the hallway's streaming light. She pulled Logan out of the shadows. He still sat in the wheelchair.

Sully passed him a bulletproof vest. "Put it on." He then helped Jennie with hers, securing it around her frame.

"Where's Cara?" she asked.

As much as Sully wanted to tell her, words didn't come. All he could do was shake his head. "Just pray. And worry about you. That's what she would want."

A small wail escaped Jennie's lips and Logan reached for her hand.

"The dogs will guard you both. There's a car waiting at the ER entrance. Follow my lead and move quickly."

No one spoke a word throughout the hospital or on the ride to the closest safe house. Sully drove the borrowed police cruiser, keeping an eye out for anyone following. As far as he could tell, they weren't being tailed.

He pulled into a rcar garage of a small medical building that acted as a front. Once inside, he took his first deep breath and let it go. *She's going to be all right, Cara.*

"Your new life begins now," he spoke to the two of them through the rearview mirror. "You both know the drill. You will receive new lives. Jennie and Logan are no more. Forget everything."

Sully opened his door and stepped out. He pulled the rear door open for Jennie to exit. But all she did was look up at him.

"Is there a problem?" he asked.

"I can't let you do it again," she said. "My sister has sacrificed her whole life for me. My new life may begin today, but you will know nothing about it."

The US Marshal stationed at this post stepped from a door and approached the car. "Is everything all right?"

"Yes, we had a breach, so I'll be starting over."

Jennie exited the car. "What he means to say is I'll need a new handler."

Sully touched her arm. "You don't know what you're saying. I need to be sure you get the life that Cara wants for you."

"I'll get the life that I make of it. The life

that Logan and I will make together. I release you of any obligation that you think you have. Tell my sister that I love her, and I will never forget the sacrifices she made for me, including giving up the love of her life. But that ends today. Now go and be with her. She would never admit it, but she needs you."

Jennie helped Logan from the car, as Sully could only stand dumbfounded at her words.

"Sir?" Logan spoke, leaning on Jennie. He offered his hand. "Thank you for everything. I can take it from here. Cara will never have to worry. I promise. Tell her wherever we land, Jennie will be safe and happy."

Sully dragged his hand down his face, half stunned and half afraid of what Cara would say. "She may never talk to me again."

Jennie giggled. "Give her time. Once she realizes what I've done for her, she'll come around. Now get back to the hospital and be there when she wakes up."

When?

Sully tried to have the same hope as

Jennie. He opened the driver's door and climbed in. He looked up at the couple in obvious love. "Goodbye."

Jennie smiled and dropped her head on Logan's shoulder. "Merry Christmas, Sully. May all your Christmases be filled with love from now on."

Sully drove out of the garage, feeling unsure of what had just happened. He radioed for an update on the hunt for Luis Morel, hearing that the man was still at large. By the time he returned to the hospital, Cara was out of surgery, alive but unconscious.

Sully entered her post-op room and stood at the end of her bed. She was still in critical condition and the doctors wouldn't know if she would make it until she woke up. He moved around to the side of her bed and took her hand. He stared at it as he ran his thumb around her palm.

"You have to come back to me," he whispered. "Wake up, Cara. I need you to tell me what to do. I find myself at a loss. After ten years of knowing that the best way to make you happy was to protect your sister, she's made that impossible now."

Sully studied Cara's sleeping face. Right now, she looked at peace. But that would all change when she learned her sister had released him from his duties. Jennie may think Cara would be grateful, but Sully knew otherwise.

He put her hand down and turned for the door. As he opened it, she spoke to him.

"She has a way of controlling a situation, with no one realizing she's calling the shots."

Sully turned quickly and approached the bedside. "You're awake."

Cara squirmed and winced.

"Don't move. You had surgery for a gunshot."

"Yeah, I figured. Now, tell me, how has Jeanette made it impossible for you to protect her?"

Sully hesitated to explain. But Cara's raised eyebrows showed impatience. "She fired me. At the safe house, she asked for a new handler and caseworker."

Cara huffed. "How ungrateful. After everything—"

"She did it for you. For us," Sully said quickly, pausing for Cara's reaction.

"What? How would her putting her life in jeopardy be for us?"

"She thinks we aren't together because of her. She thinks if I'm not her caseworker, then I won't know where she is and then we can be together."

Cara shook her head. "That's not true. You can always find out where she is."

"We know that, but she doesn't. She thinks she's sacrificing for you."

"And you let her believe that?"

He shrugged and smirked. "It's Christmas."

Cara laughed, but quickly closed her eyes in a wince. After a second of recovery, she said, "Tomorrow, you will explain to her you will still oversee her case. Understand?"

Sully nearly responded with a yes, but something stopped him. For ten years, he took Cara's orders out of his love for her, but what if compliance wasn't what she needed?

"I said, do you understand?"

"Did you ever love me, Cara?"

She winced again, but seemingly not from the pain. "What kind of question is that?"

"It's an honest question that deserves an honest answer. I have a right to know. Did I imagine our love? Was it all a lie?"

Cara dropped her gaze to the blanket covering her. "It…it wasn't a lie. It just wasn't…sustainable."

"This isn't some sort of brief on a case. There was love or there wasn't. It's as easy as that."

She lifted her chin and captured his gaze. "Love is never that easy." The pain staring at him through her eyes weakened his knees. He stepped back toward the door. "Love comes with responsibility. That's the only love that I know how to give. It's the only love that I know how to receive. I don't trust any other kind. So tomorrow, you will take Jeanette's case again. If you love me as you say you do, it's the only way to show me."

"I disagree. I love you, Cara, and it's because I do that I won't be taking Jennie's case back. You'll have no reason to deny your love for me any longer. And if you try to order me, I will quit." He turned and opened the door. "Merry Christmas, Cara."

"Sully! I'll have your badge for this!"

A glance back showed her angered and shocked expression. "You could have so much more," he said just before the door closed.

TWELVE

Cara felt useless lying in this hospital bed. Twice in a week she'd been nearly taken out. The first time, she called on Sully and he answered the call. But then, hadn't he always answered her calls?

Until today.

A tap on her door alerted her to someone about to enter. Her heart skipped a beat as she prepared for Sully to return. She wasn't sure what she would say. She needed his help. But had she pushed him too far?

"Come in," she said.

"Boss?" Chase peeked his head in. "You up for an update?"

Cara released a breath, letting her disappointment go. "Yes, have you found Morel yet?"

Chase moved to the end of her bed and

crossed his arms. "Not yet. There's a possibility he's out of the state already. We have an APB at the Canadian border and the surrounding states and airports."

Cara shook her head. "He hasn't left. He had Jeanette in his clutches. He's too arrogant to retreat now. He'll do whatever he must to get her back. If he wanted to just kill her, he would've done that at the clinic. In his weird, sick sense, he loves her. Keep the team local. I'm sorry they have to work on Christmas. I'll make it up to them."

Chase lifted his hand. "No one's grumbling. Crime doesn't stop on the holidays, and they knew that signing up." He turned to leave, but stopped. "I have Mocha. Do you want her in here with you? I would feel better knowing she's guarding you."

"Me? Morel wouldn't waste his time coming after me." She winced as she shifted on the bed. "This one's going to take some time to recuperate from."

"I'm thankful that you're okay."

She expected him to leave, but at his hesitation, she knew there was more he wanted to say. "Is there something else I should know?"

Chase frowned. "This is probably none of my business, and I'm probably the last person to offer advice, but all I know is I could have missed out on a second chance at love. Sometimes we believe we're better off alone, that we'll only get hurt if we take the risk. And maybe we will. But what if we let ourselves be loved, and it's more than we could ever imagine? What if we let ourselves love someone else, and we're better people for it?"

Cara listened intently, swallowing hard before she told her team leader that he was right, and it *was* none of his business. But she knew his confession didn't come easy. He took a risk, and it turned out well for him.

"You think I should give Sully another chance?" she asked.

Chase shook his head. "No. I think you should give yourself another chance. I don't know too much about your past, but I know you tried to love. You don't make half attempts at anything you do, and I know that included loving your father. Perhaps he didn't know how to love back, but I tell you he's the one that missed out. There's no reason for you to continue missing out as well. I know you won't regret it." Chase nodded and backed up toward the door. "I'll bring Mocha in."

Cara closed her eyes and rested her head on the pillow. She heard the door click closed and felt the tears streaming out from the corners of her eyes into her hair. Her lips trembled as her heart yearned to be loved.

But what if I get hurt? What if I can't love back? I don't want to hurt Sully.

You already are.

The realization that she had withheld her love from him for so long had already caused him so much pain. And yet, he loved her from afar.

"Oh, Sully. I'm so sorry."

The door clicked open again and Cara opened her eyes, expecting to see Chase with Mocha.

Except it was Luis Morel running to her bedside. His hand covered her mouth before she could say a word. A knife appeared in his other hand.

Cara muffled a scream beneath his grip. She tried to move her arms, even knowing she was tearing stitches from both her wounds, wounds from the hands of this man's men. He may want her sister alive, but Cara was another story. Cara's adrenaline surged as she reached for his wrist with the knife. She had mere seconds to live. With all her strength, she pulled his hand away a few inches, but nothing more. She tried to force her mouth open beneath his grip. She managed just enough to bite down on his little finger.

Morel let out a scream just as the door swung wide. The sound of Mocha's barking filled the room just before she leaped into the air and sunk her teeth into Morel's back. He swung around with the knife still in his hand and lifted his arm to bring the weapon down on the dog.

"Drop the knife!" Sully stood in the doorway with his gun drawn. If Morel heard, he ignored the command and brought the knife down on Mocha. The dog let out a piercing yelp.

Sully shot his weapon three times, and Luis Morel fell back into the chair beside Cara. His head turned her way, and she watched the life go out of him.

"Is she okay?" Cara asked, catching her breath, only concerned about the dog. From her prostrate position, all she could see was Sully kneeling over the K-9 on the floor. "Sully, tell me. Is Mocha hurt?"

Sully lifted his gaze at her. He wore a soft, encouraging expression. "She'll need some stitches, but she'll live to be a great K-9 officer."

Cara closed her eyes in relief. "Yes, I'd say she's passed the test." Cara's voice shook, and she felt her body trembling as the adrenaline escaped her and the realization that her wounds were open sunk in. "I'm going to need more stitches too."

Sully's smile evaporated, and he stood to his feet in a rush. He ran to the door and shouted, "We need a doctor in here!"

"Sully, come here," Cara said.

"Doctor!" Sully remained at the door, looking down the hall.

"Sully, come here right now, and that's an order."

He turned to her. "An order?"

Cara smiled at him. "Fine, a request. Come here and kiss me."

"What?" His mouth gaped.

She lifted a hand to him. "Please." She sounded like she was begging, and maybe she was. "Kiss me, Sully, and show me what I've been missing all these years."

His steps toward her were slow, but when his gaze fell on her lips, her eyes drifted closed, and she lifted a silent prayer of thanks to God for the second chance to love and be loved by this amazing man.

At first, Sully's touch was nothing more than a warm breath. He lifted his head just enough to capture her eyes. "Are you sure? Because, Cara, I don't know how many more goodbyes I can take."

"Me neither. But I do know I need to love you. I need to let myself give you everything I have to give. Even if it means that love isn't returned. I have to do this for myself."

"Not returned?" He took her hand and put it on his chest. She felt his fast heart rate beating against his chest. "My heart belongs to you, and it always has."

Cara closed her eyes and Sully's next kiss took her breath away. Even while nurses moved her bed back toward the operating room, Sully walked beside her with his hand holding hers until they were forced to let go of each other.

"Wait for me," Cara said.

He chuckled as his intense eyes locked on hers. "Always. You'll never be able to get rid of me again."

Cara laughed, even though it hurt so much.

"I love your laugh," he called to her as she went through the doors. "It's as beautiful as you are. You're going to marry me. Do you hear me, Cara? You're going to marry me."

Cara felt her smile grow even wider. "Is that an order, Briggs?"

He shook his head. And just before the doors closed on him, he said, "It's a promise. Because God's plans always work out to their proper end, and we were always meant to be together."

EPILOGUE

New Year's Eve promised to be the most exciting day in Cara's life. She was getting married to a man who loved her completely and whom she loved more than life itself. Sully had already put in for a transfer to DC, even though she had been willing to leave her position for him. He was having none of it, adamant that he would not stand in the way of her calling.

Now, Cara was being released from the hospital with Mocha by her side. The nurse wheeled her down to the exit to where Sully waited for her in a striking black tuxedo. Cara glanced down at her typical teal blouse and black pants and wished she had a pretty gown to wear for the ceremony.

"I thought you said this would be simple," she said. "I want to be dressed up for you too."

Sully leaned down and kissed her, lingering against her lips. All week, he had been making up for lost time, not that she was complaining. "You will be. I have a car waiting out front to take you shopping. We'll meet back up again at the church in a few hours."

Disappointment filled Cara. "I had hoped to be with you for the whole day. Are you sure you can't bring me?" They had already been apart for too long. They had so much time to make up for.

Sully lifted away from her and moved to the back of the wheelchair. He pushed her toward a black limousine in the parking lot. "I meant what I said. I'm never leaving you again. You can believe me, Cara."

"I do." She angled her head to catch his gaze, wanting him to know she meant it. "If this is what you want, I'll go buy a dress alone and meet you at the church."

"Good. But you won't be alone. Now go enjoy yourself." At the car, he opened the rear door and suddenly, her sister peeked her head out with a big smile on her face.

"Jennie!" Cara pushed forward on the chair, stunned at seeing her sister out in the open. "How? I thought you left for your new life."

"First, it's Jeanette. Jeanette Doyle." Her sister stepped from the car and flashed a diamond ring and a wedding band on her left hand. "Second, I'm free. Because of you, my beloved sister, I am free to be me for the rest of my life. I will never forget the sacrifices you made for me, and I look forward to making up for them long into our future together."

Cara pushed up to stand and wrapped her arms around her sister. Over Jeanette's shoulder, she caught Sully beaming at her with more love in his eyes than she had ever seen.

He did this.

Thank you, she mouthed to him. Tears filled her eyes.

"It's only the beginning, my love." He took her hand and led her to the car door, helping her inside. "I'll see you at the church."

Cara smiled at him. "I'll be the one running to the altar."

He leaned in and kissed her. "And I'll be the one ready to catch you. Now go buy your dress and hurry. I don't think I can wait much longer."

Cara giggled, feeling twenty years younger. Sully really had given her a second chance to love again, and she planned to love him with her whole heart for the rest of her life and never look back.

* * * * *

*If you enjoyed this story, check
out the rest of the
Mountain Country K-9 Unit series!*

Baby Protection Mission
by Laura Scott, April 2024

Her Duty Bound Defender
by Sharee Stover, May 2024

Chasing Justice
by Valerie Hansen, June 2024

Crime Scene Secrets
by Maggie K. Black, July 2024

Montana Abduction Rescue
by Jodie Bailey, August 2024

Trail of Threats
by Jessica R. Patch, September 2024

Tracing a Killer
by Sharon Dunn, October 2024

Search and Detect
by Terri Reed, November 2024

Christmas K-9 Guardians
by Lenora Worth and Katy Lee,
December 2024

*Available only from
Love Inspired Suspense.
Discover more at LoveInspired.com*

Dear Reader,

I hope you have enjoyed the Mountain Country K-9 series this year, as well as Cara and Sully's reunion story. What a joy it has been to be part of this collection, working closely with all the amazing authors who love to bring you hours of entertainment through their inspiring stories of love and intrigue. I am honored to be a part of this series and honored to bring you this Christmas story.

As beautiful as Christmas stories are, I wanted to reflect on the blessing of letting go of our expectations. There are things that we can't control and by holding on too tightly, we may miss the blessing that God wants to give us. He is the one who is in full control at all times. We can find rest knowing that His plans for us will always be good and will be brought to completion in His perfect timing. In the end, I think Sully and Cara both received a wonderful Christmas present—their own happily-ever-after.

I love to hear from readers. Please feel

free to send me an email at KatyLee@
KatyLeeBooks.com or visit my website at
katyleebooks.com.

Peace and joy to you!
Katy Lee